Richard Gordon was born in 1921. He q
on to work as an anaesthetist at St Barth
ship's surgeon. As obituary-writer for t
inspired to take up writing full-time and he left medical practice in 1952 to
embark on his 'Doctor' series. This proved incredibly successful and was
subsequently adapted into a long-running television series.

Richard Gordon has produced numerous novels and writings, all
characterised by his comic tone and remarkable powers of observation. His
Great Medical Mysteries and *Great Medical Discoveries* concern the stranger
aspects of the medical profession whilst his *The Private Life of...* series takes a
deeper look at individual figures within their specific medical and historical
setting. Although an incredibly versatile writer, he will, however, probably
always be best-known for his creation of the hilarious 'Doctor' series.

Love and Sir Lancelot

Richard Gordon

HOUSE OF STRATUS

This edition published in 2001 by House of Stratus, an imprint of
Stratus Books Ltd., 21 Beeching Park, Kelly Bray,
Cornwall, PL17 8QS, UK.

www.houseofstratus.com

Typeset, printed and bound by House of Stratus.

A catalogue record for this book is available from the British Library
and the Library of Congress.

ISBN 1-84232-502-7

1

'But I told you, he's quite a gentleman,' eighteen-year-old blonde Belinda was insisting, getting down to her sixth shampoo and set of the morning. 'His father's a Member of Parliament.'

'And my father's Richard Dimbleby.' Her friend Vi on the next-door customer was a woman of the world, well past twenty. 'Where did you meet his lordship, may I ask?'

'At the Luxor.'

'Oh, a dance-hall pick-up.' Vi wrinkled a pretty nose. Monsieur Augustin's establishment in Kensington, with its plastic Madame Pompadour decor and row of broody matrons under chromium beehives, looked exactly like every other ladies' hairdresser's in the country, and so did the little girls in pink overalls working inside. 'What's the dream boy do for a living? Or is he a millionaire into the bargain?'

'He's a scientist.' Belinda glanced proudly across the suds, scientists these days being particularly with it. 'He's ever so brainy.'

Vi snipped a pink sachet of rose-scented shampoo.

'Bet it's not long before he starts trying a few experiments.'

'I *told* you he's serious. He says class distinctions are as old-fashioned as the Tower of London.'

'Go on? One night he'll ask you back to hear his latest records.'

Belinda pouted.

'If that doesn't work he'll remember he's bought you half a dozen nylons, but left them behind on his dressing-table. Mark my words, girls have been murdered for less.'

They were interrupted by a scream from the basin, 'Are you trying to scald the skin off me, or something?'

'Zaire is something ze mattaire?' Monsieur Augustin appeared. 'A leedle too 'ot for madame's delicate complexion? *Zut!* I adjust ze temperature. Belinda, my dear, come 'ere one petit moment. You make a pig's breakfast out of that old woman's hair, you ignorant little piece of rubbish,' Monsieur added to his employee, 'and I'll kick you out of the joint so hard you won't sit down again till your Christmas dinner. Get me?'

Dismissing Vi as merely dead jealous, Belinda met her serious scientist that night as arranged, by the international clock in Piccadilly Circus tube station. He took her to a Chinese restaurant, which she thought quite dreamy, if rather indigestible. They stood outside afterwards in Shaftesbury Avenue, on a crisp December evening with all London at their disposal.

'Well,' said Randolph Nightrider. He stood on one leg, his habit in moments of emotional stress. 'Bit late for a cinema, eh?'

'We could see a cartoon programme,' Belinda suggested hopefully.

'Here, I say –' He put down one leg and stood on the other. 'Lots of people about, pushing you everywhere. I've got a car round the corner, so why not go back quietly to my place and hear a few records?'

Her inch-long eyelashes fluttered like a pair of startled sparrows.

'Besides, I've bought a present for you.'

'Present?'

'Yes. Nothing much. Half a dozen nylons. Like a fool I left them behind on my dressing-table.'

'Very kind, I'm sure,' she returned with crushing primness. 'But I don't happen to be that sort.'

'Good lord, you don't imagine I'm up to any funny stuff, do you?' Randolph looked shocked. 'We scientists are above all that sort of caper, let me assure you. By golly, yes. Besides, I thought you might like a dekko at some of my scientific instruments. They're utterly fascinating. And anyway, it's going to rain.'

His car seemed a make constructed from the spares of every other make, held together with pieces of wire.

'Don't worry, I could do the Monte in this,' he explained warmly, untying the string from the door. 'You interested in motor cars?'

'Not really.'

'They're my utter passion. Hold on to that doorknob screwed to the dashboard.'

They arrived somewhere in north London at a block of flats which struck Belinda as the cross between a church and a railway station.

'I'm afraid we'll have to be frightfully quiet,' Randolph explained, switching off. 'Lots of other important scientists live here, and they're all asleep.'

'What, at ten o'clock?'

'Yes, their brains get terribly tired during the day. You don't mind the back way, do you? Porter chap locks the front at nightfall. Security, you know,' he added darkly.

The flat threatened no seductive shades nor lurking cocktail cabinets. It was a plain monkish cell, with an iron bed, a wardrobe, and a table covered with books. Randolph carefully closed the door.

'Well, and here we are. That's one of my scientific instruments on the table. It's called a microscope. Won't you take your coat off?'

'No, thank you.'

'But aren't you rather warm?'

'No, thank you. Eeeeeek!' cried Belinda, finding herself facing the picture of a man with his head sawn in half.

'Sssssh! Quiet!' Randolph hurriedly shut the book. 'I beseech you! Are you sure you won't take your coat off?'

'Where are them nylons?' asked Belinda, coming to the point.

'Nylons? Where have they got to, now? I swear they were just here when I went out.'

'And them records?' She was admitting Vi had sense after all.

'Do let me take your coat –'

'Oh no you don't!' She wrapped it round with the air of pulling up the drawbridge. 'If you ask me you're nothing but a –'

Her suitor's jaw dropped. His normal tomato complexion changed to mashed potato. A knock had sounded at the far end of the corridor and a gruff voice came through the night, 'Warden here. Might I see if you are entertaining, Mr Forcedyke? I have reason to believe somebody is. Not guilty, I see. Thank you. Good night.'

'Not…not a word,' Randolph enjoined shakily.

' 'Ere! What is this, I'd like to know? You get me up to your flat – '

'I – I can explain everything, but not just at the moment.'

A second knock rang out. 'Warden here. Mr McWhittle, have you a visitor in your room? No, I thought it couldn't be you. My apologies. Good night.'

'The window!' Randolph threw it up. 'The fire escape's two stories below. Can you jump?'

'Jump? Are you crazy? Do you think I'm going to break my neck for some – '

'Warden here.' The knock was much nearer, like Fate catching up with Beethoven. 'Anyone in your room, Mr LaSage? I'll look for myself, if you please. My apologies, Mr LaSage. It might seem you are losing your touch. Good night.'

Randolph looked round frantically. 'Quick!' he hissed. 'The wardrobe.'

'What!'

'Belinda…my dear…my darling… ' He looked far more imploring trying to get her out of his room than trying to get her into it. 'My career…my whole life…utterly depends on you getting into that wardrobe.'

Whether it was the drama of the situation, or it being rather a lark to tell Vi tomorrow, or because she was really a soft-hearted little girl, Belinda wavered.

'I might suffocate,' she pointed out.

'A panel's dropped off the back. For heaven's sake! Hurry.'

She scrambled inside. The knock fell on Randolph's door.

'Come in! Oh…er, good evening, sir.'

'Up to your hocks in midnight oil, I see?'

'Just…just looking through a few microscope slides. Histology, you know.'

'H'm. And what might that slide be?'

'It's…it's liver, sir.'

'Allow me. Indeed? If you cannot tell the liver from the brain, young man, you may be in for certain embarrassments later in life. Anyway, you have the thing upside down.'

'Oh, have I, sir? How silly.'

Belinda heard a loud sniff.

'Do I smell cheap perfume?'

'My after-shave lotion, sir. Just spilt it.'

'You are, I presume, quite alone?'

'Alone, sir?' Randolph sounded mystified. 'But of course, sir. Why, sir?'

'It doesn't matter. I will bid you good night.'

'And a very good night to you, too, sir!'

'Here, is that an early edition of Gray's *Anatomy*? By George, I must have a look at that.'

'Take it, sir. Take it away. Please do, sir. Read it downstairs in comfort.'

'No, a glance will suffice.'

Belinda shifted slightly in the wardrobe. Something was digging into her side. She gingerly put out a hand. It was hanging from the clothes-rail, and seemed to be some sort of birdcage with a big smooth knob on top.

She screamed.

The door flew open and she found herself facing a fierce-looking red-faced old gentleman with a beard.

'Sixty seconds,' announced the old gentleman briskly, 'and you will be out in the street.'

'There's been a murder!' cried Belinda.

'It is now fifty-five seconds. Come along, young lady, jump to it. Or I shall be obliged to report you to the police for soliciting skeletons. Now you and I, my lad, must have a little chat in the morning, mustn't we? Nine o'clock sharp,' ended Sir Lancelot Spratt.

2

Randolph Nightrider will one day be a successful doctor. He wasn't very intelligent, but he had a kind heart and, as we have seen, a quick head in a crisis. Like any doctor's life, his will suffer its many instants of despair, but none so black as outside the oak door marked WARDEN OF THE MEDICAL COLLEGE at nine the following morning.

He knocked.

'Enter.'

He kept alight a little hope, like striking a match in a gale. He could hardly pass Belinda off as his sister, because Sir Lancelot had known him since birth and was, in fact, his uncle. But surely it was reasonable to have found a young woman wandering along the College corridors in mistake for St Swithin's Hospital over the road, in distress and feeling faint and looking for Casualty? The urgency of the case obliged him to sit the patient down in his own bedroom, and when people started thundering on the door he'd lost his head.

'Er – good morning, Uncle Lancelot,' he tried with a weak grin.

' "Sir", if you please. You are quite grown up now.'

'As a matter of fact, sir, I can explain everything.'

Sir Lancelot nodded. 'The girl had mistaken the Medical College for the Casualty Department, and as she was feeling faint you insisted she lay down in your bedroom. Hearing my knock, you panicked.'

"Well…that was more or less the case, sir.'

'LaSage gave me that one last week. There must be quite an epidemic of vertigo among London's young women at the moment. Though in his case,' Sir Lancelot added, 'I regret to say she was still enjoying postural treatment when I arrived.' He picked up a letter-opener like a dagger. 'Now look here, you rutting runt – oh, do stop standing on one leg – you ought to be thoroughly ashamed of yourself.'

Randolph glanced nervously round the Warden's study, a large Victorian apartment running to brass fire-irons and mahogany shelves of hand-tooled books.

'I am ashamed of myself, honestly, sir. You see, I haven't had much experience of…well, women, and all that. Not with father's views. You know, sir.'

'H'm,' said Sir Lancelot.

'I – I just thought it might be rather fun to find out,' he ended lamely.

'As a first-year medical student, I think you would be well advised to adopt some less exacting and expensive hobby, like fretwork. Why are you younger generation utterly obsessed with sex? Yes, my dear?' he broke off as Lady Spratt came in. 'I was just giving Randolph a little advice about his latest course of studies.'

'Why, hello, Randolph. Are you feeling quite well?' Lady Spratt was a little fluffy thing, against Sir Lancelot very much a pomeranian facing a bulldog. 'This arrived from the travel agent's by the morning post.'

It was a brochure showing girls in bright swimsuits sporting round a ship's swimming-pool. She laid it on Sir Lancelot's desk diary, which announced it was Tuesday, December 8th, and underneath in his own handwriting 'Twickers'.

'My dear Maud, I have no desire whatever to witness the bewitching hulas of Polynesia or the mighty Zambesi thundering down Victoria Falls,' he complained, ruffling the pages, 'and the Grand Canyon has got on very well without me. Anyway, we can't possibly plan to go away in the New Year. I am admittedly only doing this job as locum, but as sitting tenant the hospital will undoubtedly appoint me permanently after Christmas. You've already got yourself a place in the First Fifteen?' he added to Randolph. 'Well, I don't give a damn about your psychology, but I'm not going to see the Inter-Hospitals' Cup go down the drain because the team don't get a decent night's sleep. Understand? Don't let it happen again.'

'Yes, sir.' Randolph swallowed. 'Will…will that be all, sir?'

'Not quite. If you must break the rules, you must learn to do so with discretion. Last night you were as noticeable as the Salvation Army marching down the High Street on a Sunday morning. Furthermore,' Sir Lancelot ended as the door shut, 'your taste is deplorable.'

'Surely you're not serious about spending the rest of our lives in this museum?' Lady Spratt perched on the desk and lit a cigarette. 'The cook's got paranoia and the plumbing would drive a sanitary inspector to suicide.'

'I have never been more serious in my life,' declared Sir Lancelot briefly. 'The post of Warden has been graced by the most distinguished of St Swithin's sons.' He gave a brotherly nod to the busts of dead doctors over the bookcase. 'And my mistakenly resigning from the surgical staff totally cut me off from young people, which at my age can be as fatal as a fractured hip.' He fiddled with the dagger again. 'I suppose our young niece Effie rather brought that home to me when she came to stay the summer before last.'

'Very well.' Lady Spratt dejectedly gathered up the girls. 'But if you are going to stay in London, you might try and do something for Simon Sparrow.'

Sir Lancelot bristled. 'I have already done far too much for Simon. He's on the consultant staff entirely through my influence.'

'Yes, but he's broke.'

'Broke?' Sir Lancelot's eyebrows shot up. 'I should imagine his National Health salary would keep the wolf at a very respectful distance.'

'You forget he had to hang about for years on a registrar's pay waiting for the job to come up.'

'Oh, very well, very well.' Sir Lancelot rose and took a black homburg from the curly hat-stand. 'Though I fancy he and his wife are merely extravagant.'

'After all, it's Christmas,' she pointed out.

'Christmas!' grunted Sir Lancelot. 'That merely means the London traffic becomes totally impossible and all your relatives move in for a week. I'll see if I can find time for a word with Simon before leaving to watch the Varsity match at Twickenham,' he relented. 'What's for lunch?'

'Shepherd's pie.'

'I shall take mine in the hospital refectory.' He went out.

The College was built by a brewer called Turtle, who was touched by the open-handedness of the local population towards himself and returned the compliment by ploughing the profits into St Swithin's. It was founded in the last century for a hundred or so medical students to pursue their studies in an atmosphere of high principles, and remained popular with the modern ones because the board was cheap, the perks included a Christmas visit to study the scientific and hygienic methods at the Turtle Brewery, and the rules though irksome had been greatly modified – it was no longer necessary for Sir Lancelot to hold prayers twice daily or supervise the cold baths in the morning. The Warden was endowed with £500 a year, as Alderman Turtle wished him to live like a gentleman, but as none had won a pay rise since, the Warden's Lodge had developed into a convenient almshouse for the seedier members of the St Swithin's consultant staff. Everybody was happy, until that pestiferous article appeared in the newspapers.

ARE THESE BEATS OUR FUTURE DOCTORS? it asked, and described orgies with gin, gambling, and girls behind the staid front of the College on a scale quite unthinkable to the real St Swithin's students. They could never possibly have afforded it. The story was written in half an hour by a young journalist in Virtue ward for his hernia, who was told by Sister to wash properly under his arms and had his face slapped by a nurse in the sluice room. It was passed round the next consultants' meeting as though contaminated with smallpox.

'The whole thing is distasteful poppycock,' decided the Professor of Surgery, 'and these people are far too fly to be frankly libellous. Though one must admit,' he added, folding his smooth pink hands on his smooth pink blotting-paper, 'a certain laxity had been noticeable recently. I fear poor old Perris is rather past it.'

Heads nodded round the table. Dr Perris, the distinguished cardiologist, had been pensioned into the Warden's Lodge ten years ago, when he was a spry seventy.

'But Hindehead, you can't turf the old trout into a GLC geriatric unit,' objected Dr Bill Cheviot, sticking his thumbs into his canary waistcoat. Like many anaesthetists, he was of a sporty disposition. 'Who will you put in instead? A superannuated screw from the Scrubs? You wouldn't get one, not for five hundred a year. What we want is some tough old josser with cash of his own.'

'Why not Sir Lancelot Spratt?' exclaimed Simon Sparrow.

He bit his lip. As a new consultant, he'd never before dared open his mouth in the committee room. The place overawed him, with its magnificent shiny table, its guardsmen-like squads of pens, a huge clock in the corner ticking away like a pile-driver, and portraits of former consultants now staring at him from the walls, all with fixed distaste. Even his living colleagues seemed transformed round the table into stony repositories of lofty thought, though in fact one half were pondering on clinical problems up in the wards, the other half were wondering what on earth to buy their wives for Christmas, and Mr Hubert Cambridge, who always passed the time mentally playing a round at Sundridge Park, had just holed out neatly at the sixteenth. But that's how hospital business is done.

'I think Sir Lancelot should be left in peace, now he has retired to haunts of coot and hern,' disagreed Professor Hindehead quickly. He would have preferred his former colleague to have been fired into outer space, particularly as he was himself due for a sabbatical year and daren't imagine the mischief Sir Lancelot might get up to in his absence. 'Surely it is the moment to change our policy about the Warden? We should appoint a junior man with simpler needs. My own registrar, Paul Ivors-Smith – '

But the committee quickly agreed Sir Lancelot would be a capital successor to Dr Perris, this being the last item on the agenda and everyone wanting his lunch. Only one of the neurologists, with his pernickety neurologist's mind, raised the point of the post being freely advertised and applications made, with the usual thirty-four copies. Nobody decided what to do with Dr Perris himself, but a week later the poor fellow fractured his leg on the icy College steps and shortly afterwards succumbed in the wards to which he had given so much. Simon was delegated to sound Sir Lancelot on the chance of his doing a locum. The surgeon arrived from Wales by the next train.

Sir Lancelot in his homburg now crossed the road to the St Swithin's main gate, his mood like the weather, sunny but with frosty undertones.

He stopped suddenly in the hospital courtyard. Under the bare plane trees two large vans labelled ALBION TELEVISION were unloading electrical equipment with Professor Hindehead and Paul Ivors-Smith directing operations. It was the night for *Inside Knowledge*, the programme which brings you the miracles of modern surgery, a different miracle every week.

'The pantomime season would seem to be starting rather early,' remarked Sir Lancelot to the Professor as he passed.

He strongly disapproved of such revelations. His own bedside manner, moulded when St Swithin's was still a charitable institution, assumed his patients' diseases to be exclusively a concern of his own and any questions gross impertinence. This had the advantage of allowing them to recover or to die with the minimum of worry.

Sir Lancelot marched down the bright rubber-floored corridor of the surgical block, savouring its familiar smell of polish, antiseptic, and distant stewing greens. He took the consultants' lift up to Theatre D. He demanded from a nurse mask, cap, and gown. He pushed open the frosted-glass door.

Simon Sparrow's wards had yielded a light list that morning – a cold appendix, a couple of hernias, and an abdominal exploration. He put the appendicectomy on first, feeling the modern student saw a good deal of advanced cardiac surgery but nothing of the operation traditionally performed single-handed aboard ships in gales or on kitchen tables in ice-bound trappers' huts. He shot questions round the operating table, struggling like a young schoolmaster to hit the right mixture of authority and affability.

'That appendix looks perfectly normal to me,' came quietly behind him.

He glanced round briefly.

'You don't mind if I drop in?' asked Sir Lancelot.

'Not at all. I'm flattered you should join my class.'

An uncertain titter came from the students. A movement behind Sir Lancelot's mask suggested bristling of the beard.

'Who's the dresser in this case?' he demanded over Simon's shoulder. 'You, boy? Name? Don't mumble. Perkins? Well, Mr Perkins, what were the symptoms? Right-sided abdominal pain. I hope, Mr Perkins, you also examined the chest? You have doubtless heard of pain referred from the thoracic organs to the abdomen? This is not the best operation for a basal pneumonia.'

'The appendix, you will note,' Simon continued evenly, displaying the organ, 'is red and engorged.'

'Oh, that's an old one.' A syrupy chuckle came from Sir Lancelot. 'A very old one indeed. Once you apply the clamps, ladies and gentlemen, the most lilywhite appendix looks as red as a baboon's bottom. I've seen fortunes made out of that chestnut in private practice.' Sir Lancelot gave a sigh. 'No doubt we are witnessing another patient paying the penalty of being a neurotic. Do you know how to tell a neurotic from a sick man, Mr Perkins? Terribly important these stressful days to make up your mind. Psychoanalysis, you say? Dear me. You tell 'em by their underwear. Men with long woollen drawers always have a neurosis. I once had a patient with two pairs, both monogrammed. Took me half the morning to get them off. All ladies with black underwear are neurotic. I recall once a fascinating case in private…'

Sir Lancelot continued reminiscing affably. Simon sewed up the wound in silence.

'I'm absolutely sick and tired of this bad-mannered interference,' he exclaimed angrily to Bill Cheviot in the surgeons' room afterwards. 'Just because I was his student once is no excuse for him treating me like it for the rest of my life.'

'Rotten luck, old boy. I agree it's time the old battleship struck his colours and got put in mothballs. Perhaps I should have created a diversion by making alarming noises with my apparatus.'

Simon scribbled furiously in the operations book.

'Ah, there you are.' Sir Lancelot appeared, doffing mask and gown. 'I fancy I cheered up your boys and girls a little. Nothing is to be gained in teaching by solemnity.'

'Nor is anything to be gained by making the teacher look a first-class moron.'

'Oh?' Sir Lancelot's beard came up. 'Standing on our dignity, are we? Ah, well, I suppose we must bear with a little swollen-headedness from a newly-elected consultant. You are on your beam ends financially, I gather?' he added indifferently. 'I am contemplating passing some of my less complicated cases in your direction. Yet another gesture for which I feel I deserve your gratitude even if I don't get it.'

'Thank you very much,' rounded Simon briskly, 'but I'm not taking a mob of your second-class patients while busy with a few first-class ones of my own.'

The barometer of Sir Lancelot's brow fell sharply. 'Very well,' he barked. 'If you wish to cut your own throat *I* certainly shan't bother to swab up the mess. Who are you after?' he added, glaring as the Professor of Surgery appeared.

'Ah, Lancelot, there you are. There's a distinguished Czechoslovakian waiting to see you.'

'I wasn't aware there *were* any distinguished Czechoslovakians,' snapped Sir Lancelot.

'Well, here he is,' returned the Professor wearily, introducing a fat bald man with a big black moustache. 'Professor Chudik, from Prague.'

'Sir Spratt?' The Czech doctor's face lit up. 'So at last my long search is over! I am so delighted to meet you, Sir Spratt.'

'Good morning,' muttered the surgeon, shaking hands.

But the iciness of his glare had begun to melt. It is always pleasant when a colleague comes miles to see you, especially when he has to rend an Iron Curtain *en route*. It was also a neat one in the eye for Professor Hindehead.

'I shall be glad to show you anything you wish at St Swithin's,' continued Sir Lancelot loftily. 'Though I fear this afternoon,' he remembered, 'I have an urgent case on the outskirts of London.'

'And I myself must catch my plane at one o'clock,' beamed the Czech. 'I had such trouble to escape from your British Council. They so wanted to show me the waxworks.'

'Then no doubt you will want to come straight to my work on gastrectomy techniques?'

'Please?'

'My researches on the operation of gastrectomy,' explained Sir Lancelot more impatiently. 'All the specimens and papers are conveniently to hand.'

'Ah! Yes. Very interesting.' The Czech's smile broadened. 'But I am Professor of Experimental Medicine, and I have naturally come to see your famous Dr Moneypenny.'

'Dr who?' asked Sir Lancelot. 'Who the devil's Moneypenny?'

Professor Hindehead stroked a smooth chin. 'He's not on the surgical side, anyway. You wouldn't mean Dr Farthingale, would you? We have one in skins.'

'If Sir Lancelot doesn't know of him,' observed Simon, reading the notes of his next case, 'the fellow can hardly presume to exist.'

'You see, please.' Professor Chudik produced a crumpled sheet of paper. 'From your own *Archives of Experimental Physiology*.'

Sir Lancelot frowned at it.

SOME NEW ASPECTS OF MUSCLE METABOLISM WITH SPECIAL
REFERENCE TO THE NEUROMUSCULAR JUNCTION.
By Clive Moneypenny, MB, BS,
Dudley Research Fellow, St Swithin's Hospital, London.

'Oh, one of the Medical Unit wallahs,' Sir Lancelot dismissed him. 'Show this gentleman down, will you, Hindehead.'

'I'm afraid I am rather occupied with my television preparations – '

'I would feel it a great honour, Sir Spratt, if you introduced me yourself.'

'Very well, very well.' Sir Lancelot tugged his beard. 'I'll winkle him out if you insist. By the way,' he added to Simon from the door, 'you'd better have a Paul-Bunnell done on that last case. I've often seen appendicitis mimicked by the enlarged lymph nodes of ordinary glandular fever. Come along,' he directed the Czech.

'Paul-Bunnell?' Simon stared after him silently. 'Glandular fever?'

'Cheer up,' urged Bill Cheviot, who'd been pretending to read the paper. 'I've been doing the old boy's dopes for years, and you mustn't take him too seriously. No man's a hero to his valet or his anaesthetist.'

'The trouble is,' muttered Simon, biting the end of his thumb, 'it's extremely likely the old b.'s perfectly correct.'

3

'I suppose it must be extraordinarily trying, practising medicine in Czechoslovakia,' observed Sir Lancelot, marching briskly down the corridor. 'With all those commissars shooting people who won't toe the line.'

His mood had frozen over again. In St Swithin's he did not lightly afford precedence to mere Moneypennies.

Professor Chudik gave a laugh. 'We are really quite civilized, you know. We confine our shooting to birds. Just like your own commissars.'

'George!' Sir Lancelot spotted the Professor of Medicine appearing from his wards with his white-coated clinical entourage. 'Chappie from Prague here wants to meet the author of this paper.'

'Nothing could be easier, my dear fellow.' He was an affable little bouncy man. 'Moneypenny? He's metabolic, isn't he?' he asked his registrar.

'No one of that name in the lab, sir.'

'Then he's asthmatic? Or cardiac? Not one of the gout boys? Oh, Dudley Research Fellow,' he noticed. 'That's one of those obscure little experimental grants. Professor of Physiology's pigeon, I'm afraid, Lancelot. Wrong address.'

'Come along,' ordered Sir Lancelot, grabbing his visitor's arm.

The Professor of Physiology was a tall, thin, reflective fellow whose conversation consisted mainly of significant silences.

'Moneypenny, Moneypenny...Yes, I know him very well.'

He fell into contemplation of a pipette propped on his laboratory bench.

'Perhaps you would kindly allow us to share the acquaintance?' snapped Sir Lancelot after some time.

The Professor of Physiology sighed. He silently reached for the pipette. He carefully sucked some coloured liquid from a beaker. He slowly let it run into another one.

'No. I'm mistaken,' he admitted quietly. 'I was thinking of a man called Harris. You'd better ask the Professor of Anatomy.'

'Come along,' Sir Lancelot resumed the hunt. The Professor of Anatomy was brisk and busy and said he'd never heard of him.

'Come along!' commanded Sir Lancelot. 'We'll try the Professor of Pharmacology.'

The Professor of Pharmacology admitted he played golf with a Dr Moneypenny, but he was a Doctor of Divinity.

'I am a little surprised,' observed the Czech, as they hurried across the courtyard. 'In Prague, Dr Moneypenny is considered quite the world's first authority on the neuromuscular junction.'

'I'll find that damn man if it's the last thing I do,' Sir Lancelot assured him fiercely. 'Sister! Ever heard of a feller called Moneypenny?'

'Of course, Sir Lancelot.'

'Ah! Splendid.'

'He was the big portocaval shunt Mr Cambridge got in last week. Unfortunately, it didn't work.'

'Come along,' muttered Sir Lancelot.

'My time is getting rather short,' complained the Czech anxiously, looking at his watch.

'Come along!'

' 'Ere, Sir Lancelot – ' Sandilands, a thin, threadbare, grimy-looking employee with obscure duties centring round the students' lavatories, hailed him from the main gate. 'I got out your car as you said, but I couldn't put it in the courtyard because of them there telly vans.'

'For heaven's sake, man! Don't bother me at this moment with – I suppose you've never heard of a Dr Moneypenny?' he broke off.

'Course I have, sir. Ofen 'ad a pint with him across at the King George.' He shifted a home-made cigarette across his lips. 'He's got a little glory 'ole down between the boilers and the paint shop.'

'Come along,' ended Sir Lancelot.

Dr Moneypenny's laboratory was hot, small, and dark, and smelt strongly of the rats running about in their cages up by the high window. The room wasn't designed for visitors, being filled by a table covered with bits of electrical apparatus, bottles of chemicals, a glass jar of frogs, open notebooks, cuttings from journals, empty teacups, half-eaten biscuits, letters, textbooks, and a pair of socks. Sir Lancelot found the research worker himself a fair, thin young man in a polo-necked sweater and the filthiest white coat he had ever set eyes on.

'Moneypenny, allow me to introduce Professor Chudik,' Sir Lancelot announced grandly. He naturally assumed everybody in St Swithin's would know whom he was himself. 'From Prague.'

Dr Moneypenny wiped a hand on a handkerchief dirtier than his coat, and offered it.

'But Professor Chudik needs no introduction.' He gave a smile. 'The world's greatest authority on the molecular structure of acetylcholine.'

'You are so kind,' beamed the Professor.

'Won't you have a chair?' He looked round vaguely. 'I'm sure there's one somewhere.'

For the next ten minutes Dr Moneypenny and the Professor talked energetically about the mysteries of muscle metabolism. Sir Lancelot stood sullenly exchanging glances with the frogs. The discussion was so above him they might have been conversing in Czech, but this, of course, was something unthinkable to admit.

'Ahhhhhhhh!' cried the surgeon, dancing on one leg.

The pair spun round.

'Something the matter?' asked the young man anxiously.

'I should be much obliged, Moneypenny, if you would kindly get one of your blasted frogs down from my trousers.'

'That must be Ernest,' muttered Dr Moneypenny, 'I've been looking for him all morning.'

With the amphibian recaged, Sir Lancelot stiffly begged to make his adieus.

'Fascinating as I find your subject,' he declared stoutly, 'I have pressing duties of my own in the College. I hope you have a safe journey, Professor, back to your commissars. Good morning.'

'A pleasure and honour, Sir Spratt.'

'What a pong!' he exclaimed, reaching the fresh air.

Sir Lancelot blew his nose on a yellow silk handkerchief. He drew out his pocket watch. He wondered what to do next, the Warden's duties being in fact light to the point of occasional weightlessness. He couldn't possibly go home after his attitude to the shepherd's pie. He wasn't keen to prowl the surgical wards and probably run into Simon. He made his way abruptly to the red-brick Gothic building tucked beside the medical school.

The subservient black-coated librarian bowed low as he entered.

'Good morning, Sir Lancelot. And what may I do for you?'

'Morning, Miggs. I want to do a little research on nephrectomy. Kindly bring me the *Annals of the Royal College of Surgeons* for the last five years, and the relevant *Proceedings of the Royal Society of Medicine*,' he ordered.

The library was empty, and invitingly comfortable. Sir Lancelot took a big leather armchair by the electric fire. The librarian brought the books, and arranged the lamp behind his head. As he retired, Sir Lancelot opened them busily. He produced his gold pencil. He glanced quickly over his shoulder. Quietly reaching for *The Times* on a nearby table, he started the crossword.

After Sir Lancelot had briskly changed some Signore into Ignores and a Seadog into Dosage, a pleasant tranquillity swept over him. Moneypenny, Czechs, Professor Hindehead, Simon, even frogs, were dismissed from his mind. In the warmth of the fire his eyelids drooped most agreeably. Meanwhile, a few miles away at Twickenham, thirty pink and academically inclined young gentlemen were loafing about wondering if they had mere butterflies or bats fluttering in their stomachs.

Sir Lancelot jerked up and inspected his watch again. It was time for an early lunch. The first person he met outside in the courtyard was Dr Moneypenny.

'I say, I'm most terribly sorry about the frog,' the research worker began at once.

Sir Lancelot said nothing. He had to admit that Moneypenny was, after all, one of his colleagues at St Swithin's. He was still annoyed with himself failing to find any member of the hospital staff instantly. And he was intrigued why the young man's reputation should flourish on the banks of the Vltava while refusing to sprout beside the Thames.

'I've had worse things over my trousers in my time,' he dismissed it gruffly. He paused again. 'Are you taking lunch in the refectory?'

'Bit too expensive for me, I'm afraid. I usually have a beer and a sandwich across at the King George.' Dr Moneypenny stood awkwardly trying to compress a large bundle under his left arm. 'Of course, you wouldn't know what the inside of the place looks like,' he added, not particularly apologetically.

'I happen to know what the inside looks like extremely well.' Sir Lancelot was nettled. As Vice-President of everything in the hospital from the Cricket Club to the Wildfowl Society, he always treated the students' committees to beer there afterwards. As Trollope hit on it, it is sweet to unbend oneself at the proper opportunity.

The surgeon glanced at his watch again. 'As a matter of fact,' he decided suddenly, 'the King George will do admirably for a snack before driving to Twickenham. I may join you?'

The King George pub, facing St Swithin's main gate next to the College, has changed a good deal since my day. It once provided with brass lamps, frosted mirrors, and mysterious mahogany shutters, a fitting atmosphere for the thirsts of such rough characters as porters in the local market, draymen from the Turtle Brewery, and medical students. Now the Padre who so freely dispensed beer and sympathy has made a one-way crossing of the street to the hospital opposite. The rugger club photographs have been torn down. The bar has been repapered in pink with concealed lighting and a couple of Dufy reproductions. A pin-table has ousted darts, to suit the gentler tastes of another decade. Why, the place even serves coffee.

Sir Lancelot took a chromium stool, while Dr Moneypenny tried to hide the bundle under his feet.

'Hello, Pat,' Dr Moneypenny said to the pretty young red-headed barmaid.

'Hello, Clive. Your usual? Morning, Sir Lancelot. What can I get you?'

'A lobster sandwich and a glass of white wine, if you please. Pretty girl that,' he added, as she disappeared.

Clive Moneypenny looked up. 'I'm glad we find something to agree about at last. We didn't much when I was a student.'

Sir Lancelot frowned. 'I don't seem to recall your face.'

'Not unlikely,' returned Clive lightly, 'as I managed to cut as many of your classes as possible. Passing examinations without actually doing any work for them is the height of academic achievement, don't you think?'

The surgeon grunted. 'What about this research you're doing? Muscle metabolism, and so on.'

'Oh, that.' Clive ate a crisp. 'I put in for this Dudley grant when I qualified. It isn't much, and I suppose the committee awarded it because they'd never heard of me and thought they ought to have done. I never bothered pushing myself in the sports teams and the students' union and the Christmas festivities, and all that dreary stuff. I'd always been keen on physiology if anything at all, and muscle metabolism seemed a line with the fewest competitors. It's as simple as that.'

'Here we are,' interrupted Pat the barmaid, reappearing with the drinks and some clean shirts, socks, and handkerchiefs. 'Have you got your dirties?'

'Washday,' exclaimed Clive, producing his bundle from the floor.

'And here's your sub for the week,' added Pat, handing five pound notes over the bar.

'You certainly seem to have that young lady well organized,' exclaimed Sir Lancelot as she hurried away again.

Clive sipped his beer. 'Don't know what I'd do without her. I've absolutely no idea of money and such business. I simply make over my grant to Pat, and she pays me in instalments.'

Sir Lancelot bit hard into his lobster sandwich. 'Do you mean to tell me that you pay an academic grant – a St Swithin's academic grant – straight into the hands of a barmaid?'

Clive shrugged his shoulders. 'Why not? Pat's as safe as a bank, and much more fun to deal with. For a start, in a bank you never get beer – '

'If I brought this to the ears of the committee, young man, you would be in very serious trouble.'

'Oh, the committee.' He nibbled a hot sausage. 'I'm not very impressed with all you lot in the medical establishment, I'm afraid.'

'Damn you! You will kindly be civil when addressing a senior member of the staff.'

'But you're my favourite member of the establishment,' Clive went on condescendingly. 'At least you've got both the personality and the guts to be unconventional. I've had to make no end of an effort since the day I left school.'

'Which was some free-for-all rough-and-tumble establishment never teaching you respect for your elders, no doubt?' glared Sir Lancelot.

Clive ate another piece of sausage. 'I suppose that's as good a description of Eton as any.'

'Sir Lancelot!' Sandilands threw open the door. 'It's just gorn.'

'Gorn? What's just gorn?'

The lavatory attendant shifted his fag. 'Your Rolls, Sir Lancelot. I told you I couldn't put it in the courtyard. The law's just towed it away.'

'Ye gods!' The surgeon jumped up. 'What is an Englishman's liberty coming to?'

He threw some coins on the counter. He burst through the pub door. He glanced up and down the street. His eye fell on a small wrinkled man with TRAFFIC WARDEN on his cap.

'What the devil have you done with my car?'

'Wot car?'

'My Rolls, blast you!' Sir Lancelot quivered as if charged with some powerful current of electricity. 'It was here a moment ago.'

'Well, it ain't now. You'll 'ave to go to the pound.'

'How can I possibly go to any ruddy pound? I'm going to Twickenham.'

'Don't care if you're going to Timbuktu. If you wants the car back, you'll have to get it from the pound.'

'Good grief! And to think of the income tax I pay! Here, you!' His eye fell on Randolph Nightrider trying to creep into the College. 'What are you doing this afternoon?'

'I – I've a class with the Professor of Pathology, sir.'

'Damn the Professor of Pathology. You have a car? Right. Drive me to Twickenham.'

'It…it's not a terribly *good* car, sir,' Randolph explained nervously.

'I don't care if it's Genevieve's grandmother, I'm not going to miss a Varsity match. Come along! And I don't want to see any comic driving on the way.'

4

'Mrs Collpestone telephoned,' announced Miss Scutts, Simon Sparrow's demure little receptionist, that afternoon in Harley Street. 'She says she won't be keeping her appointment. Apparently, the pain in her side has gone. She rubbed some Zam-Buk on it.'

The girl arranged some letters on a desk in the corner. Simon was familiar enough with the first-floor room, because Sir Lancelot used to live in it. The surgeon had decided to turn his old house into consulting rooms, and Simon shared his with five other specialists, two half-days a week. The rent was awful, but when he'd been elected to St Swithin's a year previously Sir Lancelot had weightily advised him to take it.

'Probably as good a treatment as any, Miss Scutts,' murmured Simon washing his hands in the basin. His glance fell through the window on a smartly dressed slim man hurrying with a green attaché case to his Mercedes from the house opposite. 'That's the racket I should have tried instead of common-or-garden surgery,' he decided.

'Oh, Angus Defoe?' asked the receptionist, peering out.

'The biggest ruddy quack in London after the ducks in St James's Park.' Simon picked up a towel. 'With his little green box and his terrestrial vibrations and all that bunkum. It's a wonder what the public will put up with, as long as it comes out of a Harley Street address. You saw a countess left him a small fortune the other week? I don't suppose he did much to delay the date of collection.' He sat down at the desk. 'The new Merc. must help no end. And I had to leave my Mini round the corner when I called to see my bank manager.'

'How did you get on?' she smiled.

'Oh, very gratifying. He wouldn't shell out any cash, but he insisted on showing me his painful knee and I was able to manipulate a loose body from the joint.'

'Only one patient, this morning, I'm afraid,' she added. 'Dr Dinwiddie sent her up from Leafy Grove.'

Simon picked up Dr Dinwiddie's letter. 'Mrs Harberton? What's she like?'

The receptionist looked thoughtful. 'Just over forty and just under a hundred and fifty pounds. Wife of a stockbroker. Emerald clasp and gold charm bracelet. Nice mink.'

'H'm,' said Simon. 'Flowered curtains, do you think, veneered cocktail cabinet, and the telly disguised as a Jacobean chest? And a doorbell which goes distinctly ding-DONG.'

'No children.'

'But good at bridge.' He tossed the letter aside. 'You'd better show her in.'

'Oh, I forgot – she brought her pekinese with her. I made her leave it in the kitchen.'

Mrs Harberton paraded for Simon's inspection a regiment of symptoms including flatulence, dyspepsia, backache, dragging pain in the feet, and a feeling of heavy weights on the top of the head. He listened patiently, wondering how on earth a woman could walk about with a charm bracelet on her wrist that jangled like a goods train coming to a halt every time she reached for her handkerchief. At last the patient gritted her expensive teeth, threw out her corsage, and came to the pain in the left breast.

'That's what I went to Dr Dinwiddie about,' she explained, eyeing the carpet. 'As a private patient, of course.'

'Perhaps we'd better have a look at it,' smiled Simon reassuringly. 'If you go behind that curtain, Miss Scutts will help you off with your things.'

Simon crossed to the window and stared into Harley Street. After five minutes he realized that only a mauve silk dress had appeared over the top of the screen. He frowned. Intense mutterings were coming from behind it. After another five minutes he raised an eyebrow, and went out to answer the landing telephone.

'Well, I've managed to get dress and slip off,' announced Miss Scutts, looking pink as she appeared from the consulting-room. 'And I think I've won victory over the girdle. But I'm afraid she's a bad case of bra-addiction.'

Simon groaned. 'We can but try. After all, she's the only patient I'm likely to have this week.'

He found Mrs Harberton lying on the couch holding the sheet clutched to her neck, with the air of a lady awakening to burglars under the bed.

'Now let's get on with the examination,' he began cheerfully, deftly claiming the sheet. 'But I'm afraid you have to take your brassière off first.'

'Oh, Doctor! Is it necessary?'

'You can hardly expect me to see through brick walls, as it were, Mrs Harberton.'

'I don't think my husband – '

'My dear Mrs Harberton! Please remember I am a doctor. I assure you the whole thing is entirely impersonal.'

'Oh, very well…but, oh dear!'

The obstruction was removed by Miss Scutts. The patient lay on the couch, a quivering hand holding a lace handkerchief over her face. Nothing serious, Simon imagined. But thought was made almost impossible by the charm bracelet rattling in his anxious ears like a peal of bells on a Sunday morning.

'Please hurry, doctor,' came from beneath the handkerchief.

'I'm being as quick as I can, Mrs Harberton,' Simon apologized, 'but your charms are distracting me.'

The patient shot up. 'There! Impersonal, indeed! "Doctor", you called yourself!'

'But Mrs Harberton,' exclaimed Miss Scutts, rapidly covering up, 'Mr Sparrow only meant he was simply fascinated by the one that looks like the dome of St. Paul's – oh my God!' she cried, biting her lip.

The patient started dressing furiously.

25

'Ah, well,' murmured Simon sadly, when Mrs Harberton had shortly disappeared with a clean bill of health, 'I suppose that's the last patient I'll get from Dr Dinwiddie. I'm beginning to suspect I'm not the type for private practice.'

'I'm terribly sorry, Mr Sparrow, I really didn't think,' apologized Miss Scutts, blushing all over again.

'It can't be helped.' He reflected a moment. 'And as a matter of fact, of course, you were perfectly right.'

'There's a call just come for you on the line,' she went on, 'from the Marlborough Hotel.'

'The Marlborough?' Simon looked surprised. 'I'd better jump to it.'

'Mr Sparrow?' said a girl at the other end. 'I have Dr Sattherwaite for you.'

'What, Dr Dougal Sattherwaite?'

He whispered across to Miss Scutts the name which appeared at the foot of bulletins about the most important of people.

'Mr Sparrow?' came a voice as rich as a slice of fruit cake. 'Dr Sattherwaite here. I'd like your opinion on an acute abdomen.'

'Yes, of course...' Simon's hand felt damp holding the receiver. 'You're sure it's me you're after, not Sir Lancelot Spratt?'

'Of course it's you.' The fruit cake sounded offended. 'The patient is Miss Ann Beverley –'

'Not *the* Ann Beverley?'

'The actress, you know. How soon can you get to the Marlborough Hotel?'

'Right away,' said Simon, putting down the telephone. 'He wants me to look at Ann Beverley's belly,' he muttered unbelievingly to Miss Scutts.

Her eyes widened. 'Yes, I saw she was over here filming at Pinewood.'

Simon shrugged his shoulders. 'Lord knows why Sattherwaite sent for me. I've never even set eyes on the man. Do I look all right?'

Ten minutes later Simon drew up his Mini in Grosvenor Square, safely round the corner from the Marlborough Hotel. He knew the Marlborough to be far more fashionable than even the flashy palaces along Park Lane, and found it provided, at great cost, an atmosphere of dark polished woods, soft pink lighting, and mossy carpets suggesting the intimate luxury of an Edwardian Pullman car. A receptionist took him to the manager's office. He introduced himself to Dr Sattherwaite, a short, smooth-haired, brown-faced, baggy-eyed man, with the air of a spaniel who'd been on the jag.

'Colicky umbilical pain since ten this morning,' recited Dr Sattherwaite fruitily, pushing a button in the lift, 'with severe left-sided headache.'

'That sounds an extremely interesting case,' returned Simon, trying to measure up to the dignity of the situation.

'The temperature, pulse and respiration are slightly raised. Bowels normal. No vomiting.'

'I must thank you for giving me an opportunity of seeing the patient,' added Simon tugging his lapels, and wondering why his suit looked creased all of a sudden.

'Don't thank me. Thank Bill Cheviot. I had a rubber of bridge with him at lunchtime in Boodle's, and he seemed to think you needed an increase in practice.'

'Oh.'

A maid answered their knock at the suite.

'I will enter first, as the general practitioner,' murmured Dr Sattherwaite. 'Etiquette, you know.'

'Yes, of course… '

Simon had never seen a film star close to before, and as he glimpsed the blonde head groaning on the pillow in the darkened room he couldn't repress the curiosity and excitement to be felt by any of Ann Beverley's worldwide fans in the situation. And even if Bill Cheviot seemed to have won him the consultation in a game of bridge, he reassured himself, an astute GP like Sattherwaite wouldn't have summoned him without checking pretty carefully on his abilities.

'Who's that?' came from the bed.

'Dr Sattherwaite, Miss Beverley. I've brought the specialist.'

'I'm going to die,' announced the actress hoarsely, 'I guess you'd better send for my folks from Nebraska.'

'Perhaps we should have a little light on the subject,' declared Simon, pulling back the curtains. He was surprised to see how much older she looked. 'If you'll just answer a few questions, Miss Beverley,' he added, falling back thankfully on the comfortable clinical routine, 'we'll soon have your trouble sorted out.'

'Just to think! All this way to London, only to die.'

Simon took the history, and turned back the bedclothes.

He drew a breath. The surgeons seemed to have been playing noughts-and-crosses on Miss Beverley's abdomen.

'You've certainly had a good many operations,' he announced.

'Yeah.' The patient seemed to have recovered sufficiently from her moribund state to be inspecting him with interest. 'Los Angeles, sixty-three,' she explained indicating the scars like campaign medals. 'Chicago, fifty-nine. Grant Hospital, New York, sixty-one. Mexico City, fifty-eight.'

Simon's eyes, straying to a chair beside the bed, noticed a pile of black underwear.

'Are you going to operate?' demanded Miss Beverley.

'No, I don't think that'll be necessary.'

'That so?' The patient seemed rather disappointed.

Simon replaced the bedclothes. 'I'll tell Dr Sattherwaite my opinion of your case outside.'

'Dr Sattherwaite? Aren't you going to tell *me*, for chrissake? After all, I'm paying.'

'It's a matter of etiquette, Miss Beverley,' intoned Dr Sattherwaite.

'You're sure stuffy over this side,' she complained. 'I guess it's all those hard white collars.'

'Would you mind?' murmured Dr Sattherwaite as Simon made thankfully for the door. 'As you know, I must leave the sick-room last. Etiquette.'

'There may be some trouble from adhesions,' Simon explained in the sitting-room, 'but I really don't think she needs more than a sedative.'

Dr Sattherwaite nodded.

'If she's no better tomorrow I'll come back and see her, of course. But I could easily look in without bothering you.'

Dr Sattherwaite glared. 'The consultant attending without the general practitioner? Really! That would be most unethical. Besides,' he added, 'what about my five guineas?'

That was my dose of high life, Simon decided, making his way back to the Mini. He reflected wryly he might have earned a couple of hundred guineas by adding his own move to the noughts-and-crosses. He wondered if Dr Sattherwaite would send him any more cases. He must certainly remember to stand Bill Cheviot a drink. He opened the car door and noticed his stethoscope lying on the seat.

Simon bit his lip. In the middle of a London winter, even the most neurotic of actresses can develop pneumonia. With the strain of both Mrs Harberton and the Marlborough atmosphere, he had forgotten to examine the chest. He glanced wildly round Grosvenor Square, wondering what to do. He could hardly run back and confess to Dr Sattherwaite. He peered among the traffic, wondering if he'd see the practitioner's Rolls disappearing. His eye caught a notice saying MARLBOROUGH HOTEL STAFF ENTRANCE. He decided a patient's welfare deserved desperate measures, even to dinting professional ethics.

The man in the goods lift looked surprised, but Simon seemed to explain himself with his stethoscope. The maid in the suite told him Dr Sattherwaite had just left. He found the patient sitting up in bed sipping a Scotch-on-the rocks, watching the telly and seeming much better.

'Why, hello,' cried Ann Beverley, 'what is this? The encore?'

'I – I'm terribly sorry, but…well, you see, I think I'd better examine your chest.'

'Sure,' agreed Ann Beverley, slipping off her nightie.

'I must have a chaperon,' Simon remembered sharply.

'A chaperon? What? At your age?'

'Professional etiquette – '

'Gee, you limey doctors act as though you all work for Buckingham Palace. Or maybe you do? Liza!' she called through the door. 'Come and hold Dr Sparrow's hand.'

'Mr Sparrow,' mumbled Simon, fiddling with the earpieces.

'Mister?' Ann Beverley stared. 'But you're a doctor, aren't you?'

'I'm a surgeon.'

'I don't get it,' she announced helplessly.

'The chest seems quite clear,' Simon declared with relief, as the maid replaced the nightie. 'I'm sorry to have bothered you again, Miss Beverley.'

'Oh, any time, any time,' the actress told him amiably. 'How much is this double-feature programme going to cost me, anyway?'

'I shall probably send a bill for...for... ' Simon swallowed. 'Twenty-five guineas?' he tried.

'What, twenty-five pounds?' The patient looked shocked. 'Say, in New York it costs you that to ask a surgeon the time. Have a drink.'

'No...no thank you... ' Simon shifted his feet. 'Not while I'm working. And I must be going. Other patients, you know.'

The actress stretched lazily. 'First you might explain that mudlark on TV.'

'That's the Varsity match. Oxford and Cambridge. Like Yale and Harvard.'

'That so?' She stretched again. 'You're rather nice.'

Simon drew himself up. 'Thank you, Miss Beverley,' he returned as chillily as possible, 'but that isn't at all – '

'Professional etiquette?' She laughed. 'We're on a social level now, aren't we? Do you doctors here *have* any social life? Or do they put you in the Tower of London for that, too? How about a cup of coffee?'

Simon hesitated. 'All right,' he smiled.

He felt Dr Sattherwaite wouldn't have approved. But it's flattering for any man to have an actress like Ann Beverley inviting him even for cups of coffee.

'I don't think you Englishmen are really stuffy at all,' she confided, ringing the bell. 'It's all an act. Do you know Dirk Bogarde?'

'Only on the screen.'

'He's wonderful. I'm shooting with him right now. You're a little like him, you know.'

A whistle sounded from the television, followed by a roar.

'What's that, for heaven's sake?' asked Ann Beverley.

'No side,' nodded Simon. 'The game's over. Cambridge won fifteen-ten, I see.'

'Cambridge won fifteen-ten,' announced Sir Lancelot Spratt, stamping up the steps of the College an hour or so later.

'Mrs Grantchester's waiting,' declared Lady Spratt from the front door.

'Ah, our worthy and charming Vice-Chancellor. Sorry I'm late,' he apologized to a handsome fair-haired lady in the front hall, 'but my transport was not entirely up to the journey. And this is your brilliant daughter? In her second year at the Jex-Blake, I believe? Doubtless she will follow your example and reach the surgical staff there in time.'

Mrs Elaine Grantchester, FRCS, gave a smile. 'I think she's more inclined towards the psychological side.'

Sir Lancelot gave a grunt as he slipped off his ulster.

'I hope it's not inconvenient, Susie staying over Christmas?' asked Mrs Grantchester. 'But of course I have to go to Nigeria and John's excavating wildly in Egypt.'

'Not in the slightest, as we have one of the women's rooms vacant through illness. And, I can assure you, Elaine – ' He gave a slight tickle to his beard. 'I am very strict keeping the little lambs separated from the goats.'

Women students had floated into the College on the high tide of female emancipation after the war, but the St Swithin's authorities kept their rooms separate from the men's by an ingenious bricking up of corridors and staircases, and just to make sure allotted places only to the plainest young ladies in the medical school.

'I can leave her with the greatest confidence,' smiled Mrs Grantchester.

'Moreover, I shall keep her up to scratch on her anatomy.'

He was interrupted by a noise behind him, which was Randolph Nightrider changing legs.

'No doubt your daughter would like to see her room?' Sir Lancelot resumed.

'I'll take her bag, sir,' offered Randolph briskly.

'Mrs Chuffey is employed for that sort of thing.' Sir Lancelot glared. 'And kindly hurry off to that beastly pound place and collect my Rolls.'

'Oh. Yes, sir. Right you are, sir.'

'And furthermore, if you don't behave yourself I'll cancel our little commission job.'

'I'll have your motor back in a jiffy, sir.' That little commission job was of supreme importance to his Christmas finances.

'A glass of sherry, Elaine?' Sir Lancelot offered, as Mrs Chuffey disappeared with case and daughter. 'A pretty little girl you have there,' he added.

'Yes, Susan is quite pleasing, though terribly shy. I'm afraid I can't stay, Lancelot. University Council meeting, you know. Which reminds me, I shall have such pleasure conferring your honorary Doctor of Science when I'm back at New Year.'

Sir Lancelot gave a little bow. 'A pity you'll be missing the Ministry reception on Thursday week,' he added, opening the front door. 'Rather a trial with black tie and the trimmings, but they do these things rather well on the taxpayer's money.'

'Yes, I'm sorry to miss the fun, but one must do one's stuff for the Commonwealth. I'm sure I can trust you to look after my little Susan.'

'Implicitly,' said Sir Lancelot, shutting the door.

He went into the Warden's sitting-room. An afternoon in the open air, his flask of cherry brandy, and a gloriously exciting winning try, had combined to soften his mood since lunch, despite Randolph Nightrider's company. He grunted, glancing through the afternoon's batch of Christmas cards. He sat by the fire and reached for the evening paper.

'Not much news now Miss Debbie Dixon's disappeared from the headlines,' he observed to his wife. He ran his eye down the front page. He gathered that Ann Beverley was ill in her West End hotel, and a specialist had been called. He turned the page and found himself facing the flourishing moustache and broad grin of Professor Chudik.

RED PROFESSOR FLIES HOME, announced the paper. PRAISES OUR BACKROOM DOCTORS.

Sir Lancelot read through the caption.

" 'I have had a splendid visit,' said smiling Professor Chudik of Prague at London Airport this afternoon. 'I was honoured to meet many British doctors, including your famous research worker, Dr Moneypenny of St

Swithin's Hospital. I wish we had many men as brilliant in Prague.'
Professor Chudik refused to answer questions on East-West relations."

'H'm,' said Sir Lancelot. 'What's for dinner in Hall?' he asked, tossing
the paper aside.

'I've managed to organize you some steak.'

'That's more like it, if it's well underdone.'

'Do you want to make up a four of bridge with the Cambridges
afterwards?'

Sir Lancelot pulled his pipe from his pocket and blew through it loudly.
'No, I fancy I'll step over to the hospital. I have my gastrectomy specimens
to rearrange. Our next visitor from the communist block might possibly
be interested in meeting myself.'

Like twenty million other people in the country, Simon Sparrow and
his wife Nikki sat in their home at Dulwich that evening to watch *Inside
Knowledge.*

'How did you get on with the Medical Women's Federation?' asked
Simon, switching on the set.

'I met a battleaxe who'd retired from the Prison Medical Service and
offered me a clinic two afternoons a week in the local reform school. How
did you get on with the bank manager?'

'Like I did with that fruit machine in the rugger pavilion.'

Nikki crossed her slim legs. 'Did you see any other private patients
today, darling? Apart from that awful woman with the bra?'

Simon hesitated. He was feeling a little ashamed of himself. On
reflection, he felt that drinking coffee with your patient in her nightdress,
even if she were a world-famous film star, was not a thing you could
lightly tell Dr Sattherwaite. And now he came to think of it, was not a
thing you could lightly tell your wife. He wondered if it were a case for
professional discretion. But he gave a smile. It was stupid to feel Nikki
wouldn't understand.

'As a matter of fact, I had a most interesting half hour – '

'Ladies and gentlemen, Inside Knowledge,' announced the man brightly
on the screen. 'Now we are going over to a famous London hospital for a
programme about – this week – the gallbladder. An eminent surgeon will
be performing the operation of cholecystectomy – that is, removal of the

gallbladder – and as usual we shall be bringing this to you *live*. The doctors and surgeons in charge must, of course, remain anonymous because of medical ethics. We do not recommend this programme for young children.'

Simon's telephone rang.

'This is Envers, sir,' came his house surgeon's voice, as he picked up the instrument in the hall. 'I just thought you'd like to know the Paul-Bunnell came back negative.'

'Good,' nodded Simon. 'No glandular fever.'

'And I've just got the path. report on the appendix itself, which shows sub-acute inflammatory changes.'

'Excellent.' Simon smiled. 'By the way, Envers, how's the lady in number three?'

'I'm a bit worried, sir, particularly about the drip… '

Simon spent fifteen minutes discussing his patients. When he rejoined his wife on the sofa the cholecystectomy was well advanced.

'You will observe I have made my incision below the ribs,' Professor Hindehead's smooth tones were addressing the world in general, 'and I now cut through the peritoneal membrane to approach the gallbladder itself.'

He gave a quick glance out of camera range. Some sort of technical hitch seemed to be troubling him.

'I am perfectly entitled to come into this operating theatre or any other in the hospital,' a gruff voice came over the air. 'I don't know who you are, young man, but if you do not get out of my way instantly I shall be obliged to encourage you with the toe of my boot. Evening Hindehead,' added a burly figure in cap and mask appearing behind the surgeon. 'Don't mind if I come along to share the fun, do you?'

'You mustn't call me Hindehead,' hissed the Professor urgently.

'Why on earth not? It's your name, isn't it? Evening, Ivors-Smith,' Sir Lancelot nodded affably to the masked assistant. 'Here, I say, Hindehead, you're not going to remove *that* gallbladder, are you? It looks perfectly normal to me.'

'Lancelot! I really must ask you to withdraw – '

34

'What were the symptoms? Gallstone colic, I presume? H'm. I suppose you asked for contacts with infectious diseases? I've often seen shingles mimic gallstones before the spots appear. Nasty mess the patient might be tomorrow, eh? Itchy chest and a ruddy great slit in her belly you could drive a London bus through. I remember once a very interesting young lady in Brighton – '

A card appeared saying that normal service would be resumed as soon as possible.

'Well, at least with me we weren't on the air,' said Simon, rising and switching off. 'Let's go to bed.'

As he was dropping off to sleep it occurred to him he still hadn't confessed to Nikki about Ann Beverley in her nightie. 'First thing in the morning, definitely,' he murmured to himself.

5

It was Thursday morning the following week. The clock on the St Swithin's main gate struck six. Sir Lancelot opened his eyes in the darkness. He gave a grunt. He strained his eyes towards his wife, snoring faintly on the next pillow. Gently and silently he crept out of bed.

He fumbled on the chair for his tartan dressing-gown, necessary because it had been snowing during the night, the windows were wide open, and he refused to have central heating in his bedroom. Contemplating again for a moment the form of Lady Spratt, with bare feet he stealthily crossed the room.

He turned a knob. After a few moments came the noise of jet fighters, followed by screeching geese and cackling chickens. Then a flat Australian voice suddenly flooded the room with summer sunshine.

'It's a wonderful afternoon here in Sydney,' said the voice.

'Wheeeeeeeeee!' went the set.

'A capacity crowd and the Hill jam-packed with spectators – '

Sir Lancelot turned up the volume.

'Here comes Murchie, the young fast bowler who's done so much for Australia today. He's starting his run now – Wahwah! – Strongi'th'arm at the other end hasn't opened his score... Murchie's running up... What a beauty! He's out! Caught in the gully! England are six wickets down for only ninety-four runs, and my word are they in dire trouble!'

'Bah!' said Sir Lancelot, switching off the radio.

Lady Spratt sprung up in bed.

'Why the devil we don't send eleven Girl Guides out there to play 'em and have done with it, I don't know,' he added fiercely as his wife switched on the light.

'You woke me up,' she complained.

'I think I could do with a cup of tea,' he announced, taking no notice.

'By the way, Lancelot – ' She adjusted her hairnet, 'I knew I'd something to ask you last night. Don't you think we ought to have a child?'

The surgeon stared at her. 'Good grief, woman, are you out of your mind? I don't know if you're feeling your age, but I certainly am.'

'I mean a child for Christmas, you fool. You saw that scheme in last night's paper. You take a child from a poor home and give it a decent holiday.'

Sir Lancelot pulled his dressing-gown cord. 'We've already got young Susan, and the entire Nightrider tribe are moving in on us.'

'But the place will be frightfully empty with half the students away. I think it would be a Christian act.'

'Oh, very well, very well,' he agreed shortly. 'I'll ask the Almoner if she can find us a clean and respectable one. Go down and get the tea, will you? You know I can never manage that blasted gaslighter.'

After his tea, Sir Lancelot withdrew to the bathroom. He lay amid the steam in the huge Victorian tub, he soaped his hairy chest, and he played a little game he was rather fond of balancing the cake of soap on the end of his toes. Sir Lancelot spent a good deal of time in his bath, believing everybody was entitled to one sensual experience per day and this got it over as early as possible. His thoughts strayed from the shortcomings of English batsmen in the Antipodes to a more pleasant contemplation of the reception that evening. Unlike some London surgeons, who make after-dinner speeches so regularly you wonder how they ever manage to raise their families, Sir Lancelot was not a party enthusiast. But he felt the Ministry do would be fairly agreeable. After all, the host was a pleasant sort of chap and it was being held in a perfectly decent place.

About the time Sir Lancelot was vigorously towelling himself, Clive Moneypenny was eyeing the card on his mantelpiece which had arrived the previous Monday morning.

> HIS GRACE THE DUKE OF LANCASTER KG, PC, GBE,
> Requests the Pleasure of the Company of
> Dr Clive Moneypenny and Lady
> at a Reception by the Ministry of Science
> on Thursday, December the Seventeenth
> at Nine o'Clock
> in the House of Lords
> Black Tie   RSVP   Carriages at two a.m.

'Better late than never,' he murmured, sticking it back among a jumble of cigarette packets, test-tubes, pieces of string, half-eaten bars of chocolate, dissecting instruments, broken pencils, paper scribbled with formulae, and bottled dead frogs.

'I suppose it was the moustached Czech,' he addressed himself in the cracked mirror. 'I see the gentleman in the Ministry – "Valerie, my dear, *who* is this doctor with the funny name all over the evening papers? But Valerie, he's *frightfully* famous, it says so in black and white. I know Valerie dear it's the Russians or whatever they are who say so, but they always seem to know *far* more about our people than we do. Put him on the list for Thursday, Valerie, there's a good girl. And bring me my coffee, with two chockie bikkies" Ah, well,' Clive added, starting to shave, 'never look a gift canapé in the mouth.'

After wasting some time finding his polo-necked sweater under a pile of books, he dressed and went down for breakfast.

Clive lived in the Shangri-La Hotel, which afforded fine views of the British Museum and catered for drunk Scotsmen missing the night trains from King's Cross, the seedier commercial travellers, a few old ladies with nowhere else to go, and one or two mysterious silent men who went out very late at night and came home very early in the morning. There were twenty-odd rooms and Clive lived on the top floor, which was convenient both because it was cheaper and his landlady suspected he practised some form of black art, possibly with live babies.

'Fenella, you look perfectly ravishing this morning,' he announced, sitting at his little table in the corner, with its grubby cloth and pair of pink paper roses in the flower-vase. 'Would ye be after rustling me up a couple of nice fried eggs, now?'

The pretty waitress smiled. 'You know I'd give you all the eggs in the world if I had them. But it's only the bacon.'

'Fenella – wouldn't you like to go to the House of Lords? In a beautiful silver dress with glass slippers and a golden coach drawn by six milk-white horses?'

'Oh, Doctor! You have the blarney, sure you have.'

'Don't be too cocky, Fenella. I may have a magic wand in my room. It's that streaky stuff, I suppose? Morning, Mrs Cheevers,' he called across the dining-room. 'How's the back? I'm so glad. Here again, Mr Plumpton? Things still brisk in the monumental masonry line, I hope?'

Clive propped *The Molecular Structure of Nuclear Enzymes* against the vase, and started to read.

'Dr Moneypenny,' he was interrupted after a few lines. 'Can you come to my office after breakfast?'

'Ah, Mrs Brewis.' He inspected his overweight landlady. 'I'm afraid I'm in the most frightful rush getting to the hospital.'

'What I have to say I shouldn't like to in public.'

'I have no shame, Mrs Brewis. Say on.'

She lowered her voice. 'It's about my rent.'

'What? Didn't I give you the cheque last Monday? How stupid of me.'

'No, Dr Moneypenny. Nor the Monday before. Nor the one before that. I have to live, Dr Moneypenny.'

'How I agree with you, Mrs Brewis. I'll see you get a cheque tomorrow. My secretary will send it. She becomes rather occupied with other duties near Christmas.'

'If not, I'm afraid you'll have to vacate – '

'Would you like to go to the House of Lords, Mrs Brewis? To dance all night through the marble halls to the music of hidden strings? To share the laughter of beautiful and extremely well-mannered young ladies – '

'By tomorrow, Dr Moneypenny,' she snapped. She would gladly have given three weeks' rent to get rid of him. And that Fenella would have to go, for a start.

Clive returned to his book with a sigh. The streaky bacon was cold, but he didn't notice it. He'd forgotten about both the rent and the reception by the time he was walking across Bloomsbury to St Swithin's, his mind being filled with the problems of nuclear enzymes. Crossing the road to the main gate he was almost run over by a shiny new-looking grey Rolls-Royce.

'Sorry,' called a pink-faced young man at the wheel. 'But you ought to look where you're going, by golly.'

'Wasn't I?' returned Clive amiably.

'Might have been a nasty mess.'

'Oh, I expect I'd clean off very easily.'

Randolph Nightrider touched the accelerator and drove towards the West End.

Twenty minutes later he parked beside a row of plate-glass windows, behind which beautiful and constantly-polished cars were displayed with the elegance of the latest creations in Hardy Amies.

'Good morning, sir,' Randolph was greeted by a bright young man with a gardenia. 'And what can I do for you?'

'I'd like to see Colonel Cling, if it's OK. I'm Mr Nightrider.'

'He's with a client, sir, but I'll see.'

'Mr Nightrider?' drawled the Colonel, resting his foot lightly on the bumper of a Silver Cloud. 'Oh, that terribly nice young man. Would I be a bore if I asked you to excuse me a moment?' he asked his customer. 'Know his family well, and that sort of thing. Father's in the Government, y'know. 'Ullo, me old china,' he added to Randolph outside, neatly changing gear with his accent, 'and what little bit o' villainy are you up to?'

Randolph, who had a knowledge of the second-hand car market beyond his years, knew Colonel Cling out in Notting Hill, before his promotion.

'I've got a stone bonker, Clingy,' he announced proudly. 'See this motor car – two thousand miles on the clock, electric windows, cocktail bar, stereo radio. Belongs to an old gaffer who's fed up having it towed away, and is getting something more pocket-sized for London. I convinced the gaffer last week I knew a thing or two about motorcars, and in the end he asked me to sell it. On a ten per cent commish,' Randolph ended, slapping his chest.

'I'd go to three thou,' murmured the Colonel.

'My dear Clingy, don't make me laugh.'

'I mean, I'd put three on the receipt and we could split the resale profit.'

'The old gaffer's thought of that,' admitted Randolph ruefully. 'He wants to see the customer's cheque.'

The Colonel fingered his Guards tie. 'See here, china, I'll do you a favour. A party rang up this morning looking for a low-mileage Rolls. Name of Twelvetrees. Here's the address. Drop round and see if you can do business.'

'I say, Clingy, that's decent of you,' Randolph told him gratefully.

'Think nothing of it. It's Christmas, ain't it? Besides,' added the Colonel, 'I'll be wanting a hundred nicker for the intro.'

The address was a mews off the King's Road in Chelsea. It had stopped snowing by the time Randolph stopped opposite a neat little house, and the sky-blue front door glistened prettily in the winter sunshine. He rang the bell. An upstairs window shot up, and a bald, fat face appeared, half covered with lather.

'Yes?'

'I'm from the motor – '

'That the wagon? Be down in a minute.'

Mr Twelvetrees finished his shave and appeared in a fur-collared jacket, smoking a cigar.

'You'll find this an absolutely splendid motor car,' Randolph started warmly. 'Two thousand miles on the speedo, one very careful owner, electric windows – '

'OK, OK.' Mr Twelvetrees seemed one of our brisker businessmen. 'Can a lady handle it?'

'Can she indeed, by golly!' Randolph administered a reverent pat to the coachwork. 'Power-assisted steering, fully automatic gearbox – '

'I'm giving it my niece for a Christmas present,' Mr Twelvetrees explained briefly. He directed a nod at the house. 'She lives here. How much?'

'Six thousand.'

'Four.'

'Five.'

'OK. Cheque suit you? Or do you want it in cash?'

Randolph leant against the blue doorpost. He was trying to work out ten per cent of five thousand pounds, less a hundred for the intro. Arriving at the figure, he felt it was quite the most wonderful thing that could happen in his life. But he was wrong.

'My niece,' nodded Mr Twelvetrees shortly, busy with his cheque book on the bonnet.

'Why, it's an absolutely *darling* car! Hello.'

The girl Randolph found himself facing was more beautiful than any he could possibly think of, and he spent most of his waking hours thinking about them, at that. She had long black hair and soft pouty lips and was wearing a mink coat over a nightie. A faint, sensuous perfume tickled his nostrils.

'Hello,' returned Randolph, repressing an impulse to make a noise like a barking seal.

'But what a gorgeously lovely Christmas present!' The girl's eyes sparkled. 'I simply don't deserve it.'

'Course you do,' declared Mr Twelvetrees. 'Every nut and bolt of it. Want a demonstration run? The salesman here will fix it.'

'Urk! Yes, of course,' said Randolph.

'Just to show me how the knobs work,' agreed the girl. 'How about lunchtime?'

'By golly, yes!' His face fell. 'Though I'm rather tied up at the – with appointments till two-thirty.'

'Three o'clock, then? It'll still be light for an hour.'

'Urk.'

'I beg your pardon?'

'Yes, of course. Back here at three. Jolly good. Well, goodbye for now.'

'Hey!' called Mr Twelvetrees. 'You've forgotten your cheque.'

Randolph dazedly took a bus back to St Swithin's. He wished he could have given a demonstration on the spot, particularly as his unavailability at lunchtime was due not to academic duties but another complication in his otherwise dispiritingly simple life.

The College traditionally gave a play in the hospital Founders' Hall every Christmas Eve, and as this date was now just a week away everyone felt it time to start rehearsals. A murder mystery had been chosen, whose title I shall not reveal, out of respect for the author. The only difficulty was casting, which was complicated that year by the presence in College of Susan Grantchester.

We have seen that Susan was a pretty girl, but a shy one. When your mother is a leading consultant surgeon, Vice-Chancellor of the University, chairwoman of a dozen important committees, and with a personality in the megaton range, you haven't much option about the shyness. Susan was as full of bubbles inside as a bottle of champagne, and once the cork was removed she hit the ceiling. She seemed to have packed a do-it-yourself Cleopatra kit in her suitcase. All week she'd been striking languid attitudes round the College or sidling about with such a mysterious heavy-lidded look she was a mass of bruises from bumping into the furniture. This naturally attracted attention, and not only from Randolph Nightrider.

'Right, ladies and gentlemen,' McWhittle had begun at the casting meeting in the common room the previous Saturday. 'I take it I'll be producer as usual? The first character to cast is the Girl. Quite frankly, I don't really think Susan would be right for it.'

McWhittle was a little, brisk, sandy man with hair sprouting from all sorts of surprising places on his face. Like many seriously studious youths, when he fell for Susan he went like the old Eddystone lighthouse. He'd even spent ten shillings buying a potted azalea to brighten her room and, he hoped, her life.

'Why not Susan?' objected everybody at once.

'Matter of type-casting,' he mumbled, surprised at the opposition. 'After all, you wouldn't want Jayne Mansfield to play Hamlet's mother.'

'Why not?' cried everyone again.

McWhittle conceded defeat. 'Well, anyway, I don't think Terry LaSage is the slightest bit suitable for the Lover.'

'Don't you, dear boy?' lightly observed LaSage, who had sidewhiskers and monogrammed shirts.

'I know you were a hit as the Commander in *French Without Tears*, Terry. But we want someone who can seem a real cad with women.'

Loud laughter.

'Honestly, ladies and gentlemen,' McWhittle struggled on, determined that LaSage of all people shouldn't get his hands on Susan rehearsing every day for the following week, 'I think he'd be a flop as a lover.'

Uproar.

'If Terry's the Lover, that leaves us with Susan's husband,' he ended grimly.

Randolph Nightrider was cast by acclamation. As he was killed in the first ten minutes McWhittle didn't mind too much.

The first rehearsal was called for lunch hour on the day Randolph sold the Rolls.

'We've got to be perfectly serious about this entertainment, ladies and gentlemen,' McWhittle was addressing the stage as Randolph turned up breathlessly. The producer tugged at the Fair Isle sweater he was wearing with dark glasses for the occasion. 'It may be a slight little piece, but everything's got to be utterly lifelike, even the corpse. I mean, perfectly convincing,' he added as the cast guffawed. 'Right from the moment of curtain up. And for Lord's sake don't forget for a moment Slasher Spratt will be sitting in the front row. Right, everybody. Overture and beginners, please.'

The first heavy scene, which involved Randolph tippling from an imaginary whisky-bottle on an imaginary sideboard, opened with Susan appearing through the imaginary French windows daintily flicking an imaginary riding-crop.

'I don't think that entrance was *quite* it,' counselled McWhittle from the stalls. 'Here, let me come up and show you.'

He spent the next five minutes moving her about the stage with his own hands.

'Right,' he announced. 'Now Randolph enters upstage centre, looking eager.'

'Like this?' asked Randolph Nightrider.

'Don't stand on one leg, old man. You're not playing a stork.'

'Oh, right ho.' Randolph raised his voice. 'Who else?' he demanded towards Susan.

'Is that you, darling,' she replied.

'Other way round,' complained Mr McWhittle.

'Oh, sorry, old cock.'

'Is that you, darling?'

'Who else?'

'That's better. Go ahead.'

Looking more eager, Randolph embraced her.

Susan screamed.

'Here, I say.' McWhittle frowned. 'That's not in the script.'

'He bit me!' cried Susan, holding her lip.

'Most frightfully sorry. Did I really? Perfectly accidental, I assure you.'

'Steady on,' muttered McWhittle thickly.

'Well, you told us to make it convincing,' Randolph pointed out.

'Perhaps you could sort of kiss her hand, or something, for rehearsals?' the producer suggested.

'Oh, I don't mind,' declared Susan bravely, taking another look at Randolph. 'I mean, it's all part of the play isn't it?'

'You won't kiss Susan in rehearsals,' persisted McWhittle gruffly.

'I'm not sure if I quite like that.' Randolph went a little pinker. 'I'm the actor, by golly, and I can play the part as I like.'

'Oh? And *I* can cast someone else.'

'All right, it's a pretty miserable part and I have things to occupy me in Town at the moment. I shall confine myself to looking after the props instead. Goodbye, Susan,' he added, playing the line better than his earlier ones.

He fancied he saw a tender glance in her eye as she nursed her cut lip while he strode haughtily to the wings. But, he told himself wickedly, what price Susan now? There was an altogether more delightful fish in his aquarium.

'And here I am,' he announced in the mews, as Chelsea Parish church struck three. 'Where shall we go?'

'A little run in the country would be lovely,' suggested the girl in the mink, settling in the passenger seat.

'I'll get her up to the ton on the Barnet by-pass,' promised Randolph, releasing the brake.

For a second the vision of Susan shimmered beyond the windscreen but faded. 'Wonderful motor car,' he added lovingly. 'Jolly generous of your uncle to give it you for Christmas, I must say, Miss Twelvetrees.'

'Oh, yes.' She gave a little laugh as they moved off. 'Don't call me Miss Twelvetrees. Just call me Debbie.'

6

'Miss Ann Beverley's suite, please,' Simon Sparrow asked the girl behind the reception desk at the Marlborough Hotel later that afternoon.

'The page will show you up, sir.'

'Oh – and is Dr Sattherwaite waiting?'

'Dr who, sir?'

'I expect he's up there already. Thank you.'

Simon gave her a smile and made for the lift.

Ann Beverley opened the door herself. She was wearing a tight, bright yellow jumper and slacks, and looked as bewitching as Titania.

'Why, hello, Doctor! Or is it hello, Mister?'

Simon felt relieved. All across London he'd worried he'd made a mistake in diagnosis and would find an actress with roaring peritonitis.

'Dr Sattherwaite sent for me,' he began, going inside.

'Oh, that guy. No, I sent for you.'

'*You* did?' Simon stared. 'But that's really most unethical,' he told her quite severely.

'Aw, gee, those ethics are growing in again.' Ann Beverley sighed and flopped on her sofa, highly decoratively.

'They're rather useful, you know,' Simon persisted. 'They save a good many demarcation disputes.'

'Let's just call it a social visit,' decided the actress. 'Does that make you less scared? Or do your ethics impose conversational chastity?'

As she waved him to a chair he suddenly remembered he'd somehow not yet told Nikki of his earlier visit.

'Why on earth did you send for me?' he asked.

'One, because I like you.' Ann Beverley fitted a cigarette in her gold holder. 'Two, because I want to ask you about my vibrations.'

Simon frowned. 'Your what?'

'My terrestrial vibrations.' She looked surprised. 'I guess you know all about them? You're a doctor.'

'I'm afraid that's something I must have missed in medical school.'

'Well, Dr Defoe sure knows about them.'

Simon jumped up. 'Dr Angus Defoe? From Harley Street? Surely you don't go to him?'

Ann Beverley raised her well-drawn eyebrows. 'Why ever not? All the rest of London does.'

'He's not a doctor,' declared Simon hotly. 'He's simply an unprincipled quack.'

She looked more surprised. 'You don't say?'

'The man's an utter charlatan. A rogue. A danger to the public.'

'But he measured my terrestrial vibrations,' she objected. 'He said they were the strongest he'd ever seen.'

'That's all so much bunkum! You might just as well start treating people with spells and magic circles, eye of newt and tongue of frog, and that sort of thing.'

'He measured them with his little green case – '

'Which, of course, is no use whatever.'

'Oh?' She lit her cigarette. 'Why not?' she asked calmly.

'Why, because…' Simon came to a halt. He shrugged his shoulders. 'It's impossible to say easily,' he added uncomfortably. 'But it just isn't, that's all.'

'Huh-huh!' She gave a laugh. 'There's the Doctors' Union talking again.'

Simon bent over her. 'Miss Beverley – you are an intelligent and highly world-wise woman. If I have done nothing else for you, please let me leave here feeling I've warned you off this Defoe fellow for good and all.'

'But I don't *want* to be warned off him.' She looked slightly offended. 'He's very charming.'

'Miss Beverley, with an abdominal history like yours, any day you're likely to get something acute and you'll send for him instead of a doctor. By the time the damage is discovered, it'll be too late.'

'Well, now! That's a happy thought.'

'But it's true. Will you promise me to get rid of him?'

'OK, OK.' She got up from the sofa. 'I guess you wouldn't get so worked up about it if you didn't mean it.'

'It's only your welfare I'm thinking of.'

'Sure it is.' She gave a smile. 'Care for a drink?'

'I'm afraid not.' He felt faintly surprised with himself for the outburst. Now he must go quickly. Last time he had been unwise – indeed rather naughty. 'Besides, I've a rather pompous party ahead later this evening,' he added apologetically, fearing he seemed impolite.

'I'll see you down.' She opened the door. 'I've got to chivvy the desk about an extra bedroom over Christmas. You don't mind sharing a lift with me? Or would you rather have a chaperon?'

Simon laughed. He was relieved to be leaving, and it is faintly flattering for a young surgeon to share a lift with a famous actress, on personal rather than professional qualities. He was still laughing with her as he crossed the hall to the front door, where, as actresses have a pleasant tendency, she lightly kissed him goodbye.

'Well!' exclaimed Deirdre Ivors-Smith behind the *Queen*.

Deirdre had just said goodbye to three of the consultants' wives whom she'd asked to tea at the Marlborough, to plan the St Swithin's Christmas Jumble Sale for the following Tuesday afternoon. She'd found the tea-party most agreeable. She may have been a mere registrar's wife but she'd drawn the best ticket for years in the hospital marriage lottery. Paul Ivors-Smith was the son of a City broker, and so rich that it sometimes made him feel in St Swithin's quite uncomfortably embarrassed, a suffering that his wife happily did not share.

'Mr Ivors-Smith's car is outside, madam,' announced the porter, approaching.

'Thank you.' She threw aside the *Queen*. 'Tell me, Porter, who is that blonde woman in trousers talking at the reception desk?'

'But that's Ann Beverley, madam.'

'Well!' said Deirdre Ivors-Smith again.

She climbed into the Lagonda while Paul patiently waited for the traffic to move.

'Well!' she repeated. 'What would you say if I told you Simon Sparrow and Ann Beverley were playing a love scene in public a couple of minutes ago?'

Paul laughed. 'I'd say it was really Sir Lancelot Spratt and the Matron.'

'They were.' Deirdre tightened her lips. 'Right here on the hotel steps, kissing away like mad. I was only a yard off in the hall.'

Paul raised his eyebrows. 'Go on?'

'Simon Sparrow, with his dear little dreary house in the suburbs and his dear little dreary wife.'

She gazed with great satisfaction through the stationary windscreen. Had it not been for Simon she too would have been a consultant's wife. Paul and he were up for the job at St Swithin's after Sir Lancelot resigned, and Simon had won.

'We'd better keep pretty quiet about it,' Paul suggested earnestly.

'Quiet?' She looked amazed. 'Why?'

'Well...' Paul stroked his weak chin. 'I mean it's not the sort of thing you'd like bruited about.'

'Oh, you men!' She stared through the windscreen again. 'By the way, you'll have to go to Hartnell's before they shut.'

'Oh, lord!' Paul groaned. 'You know what parking's like, especially before Christmas.'

'You don't expect me to go to the reception tonight stark naked, do you?'

'You might have collected the dress earlier.'

'I'm not wandering about London lugging huge great boxes,' declared the former chatelaine of men's surgical. 'Why don't we get a move on?'

'How the hell can I, with this ruddy great grey Rolls blocking the road?' returned Paul crossly.

Sometimes he yearned for those days in the ward when he gave the orders.

'Now it's shifting,' she ended. 'It seems to be driven by an idiot.'

'Ah, there's a gap,' exclaimed Randolph Nightrider in the car ahead. He dexterously ran the Rolls into it. 'Five thirty,' he announced. 'Just the time for a drink, Miss Twelvetrees. Debbie, that is.'

He helped her out, with some ceremony.

Susan had vanished from Randolph's mind as completely as Sir Lancelot himself as he ushered Debbie into the soft-lit bar of the Marlborough. It was going to come jolly expensive in this place, but by golly! he told himself with the commission on the Rolls he could splash it about a bit, and still satisfy his ambition of buying a second-hand MG. Like many more perceptive men, he sensed as they sat down the importance afforded by an accompanying beautiful woman. Even crossing the hall with Debbie, everyone had simply stopped and stared at her.

'Well,' began Randolph, as the waiter brought a couple of martinis. 'I hope you enjoyed the ride?'

'But it was fabulously exciting! Especially when you just missed that petrol tanker.'

He shuffled his legs under the table.

'But if you're not really a car salesman,' she asked, 'what do you do workwise?'

'Oh, I'm a sort of scientist,' Randolph explained automatically. 'My father's a Member of Parliament.'

Debbie raised her eyebrows. 'Really?' She sipped her martini. 'Do you happen to know Lord Mewson? Or Lord Chingford? Or the Earl of Epping?'

'You've had connexions with the aristocracy?' asked Randolph with interest.

'Oh, many,' said Debbie.

She lit a cigarette.

'It was a jolly nice day, I must say,' announced Randolph warmly, gulping half his martini at once. 'Pity, really, it's got to end.'

Slowly emitting smoke from her pouty lips, Debbie inspected his frank features, open to the point of vacancy.

'Like to come to a party?' she mentioned.

'A party?'

Debbie nodded. 'Yes, the Glendowers. Christmas cocktails. Sevenish. There might be some funny people.'

'By golly.'

'Good,' said Debbie, taking this as acceptance. 'It's hundreds of miles away in Hampstead somewhere, so you can drive me. I suppose you can change pretty quickly into a dinner jacket?'

'Like a flash.'

'Take me home first, dear.' She touched him on the cheek. The pouty lips opened. 'You know, you're very sweet.'

Somehow Randolph managed to drive the Rolls to Chelsea. His endocrine glands, so often likened to an orchestra, were playing so *fortissimo* he couldn't hear himself think. This delicious female had walked into his life in a mink coat and a nightie only that morning, and here she was inviting him out to parties. By golly! he told himself, trying to negotiate Hyde Park Corner. I must have a good bit of the old what-it-takes after all, eh? As for dear little Susan, she was the nursery slopes compared with the Cresta Run.

As he drew the Rolls up in Debbie's mews, the front door was opened by a small elderly man in a blue suit with a big red carnation.

'My uncle,' smiled Debbie. 'Another one. See you when you've changed.'

Randolph drove back across London to St Swithin's, his mind occupied with the possibility, among many others, of sneaking in and out of the College without being spotted. He parked the Rolls several streets away, crept up the back stairs, and shakingly drew his dinner jacket from the wardrobe in which Belinda had passed such a *mauvais quart d'heure*. Slipping it on, he peeped out of his bedroom door. He remembered all the students and Susan would be rehearsing. He tweaked his black tie, hurried down the back stairs again and sprinted for the car like a maniacal gazelle.

As Randolph reached the bright blue front door, the man with the red carnation was leaving.

'Chilly night,' Randolph greeted him heartily. 'Does to keep well wrapped up.'

But Debbie's uncle seemed disinclined to reply.

Randolph shut the door behind him and cried, 'Haloooo!'

'Come on up to the sitting-room,' Debbie's voice floated down the narrow stairs.

He found her wandering about smoking a cigarette, in her black underwear.

'Urk,' he said.

'I was just changing,' she explained.

Randolph stood on one leg.

'Randolph... ' Debbie crossed to him with a smile. 'You really are very sweet.'

She put her arms round his neck and kissed him.

'Would you like to stay with me tonight?' she enquired.

'By golly!' cried Randolph, for a moment not standing on any legs at all.

'Now we've got to go to the party,' continued Debbie, releasing him. 'Everything in its proper time and place, don't you think?' she added with another smile. 'Come and help me do up my zip.'

There was hardly room in the Glendowers' front drive at Hampstead for Randolph to park Debbie's Rolls among all the others. The house was blazing with lights, quivering with noise, and seemed jammed to the ceilings with people.

'Why, here's Debbie!' cried everyone, as she led her escort, rather dazed, into the hall. 'It's Debbie! Hello, Debbie! Wonderful to see you, Debbie!'

Randolph reflected she seemed a popular girl.

'Let me introduce myself – I'm Harry Glendower.' A sporty-looking fat fellow in a crimson cummerbund appeared as Debbie was swallowed in the crush. 'I say, is that your Rolls just past the conservatory?'

'Yes, it is, actually,' Randolph admitted modestly.

'You're a lucky young man,' the host assured him heartily. 'It's the new high-compression job, isn't it? I've been trying to screw one out of my dealer for months. And you're a friend of Debbie's, too?'

'Well, actually, yes.'

'I say, you *are* a lucky young man!' He slapped Randolph on the back with a chuckle. 'Champagne?'

'I say, thanks.'

Randolph stood grinning into space over his glass. This, he felt, really was seeing life and no mistake. He'd never enjoyed himself so much. But all the same, he found he kept looking at his watch to see how the time was passing.

'Here's a dear, dear friend of mine,' announced Debbie, descending on him. 'His name's Randolph.'

'Is he a millionaire?' asked someone at the back.

'No, but his father is.'

This brought roars of laughter. Randolph gave a weak smile.

'He's terribly sweet and I won't have any of you girls trying to pinch him,' announced Debbie, giving him a pat on the cheek.

Randolph smiled again. He took another look at his watch. The evening seemed to be going awfully slowly.

'Yes, you're a lucky lad knowing Debbie,' repeated Harry Glendower, as he and Randolph suddenly found themselves alone again. 'I mean, London really does get so terribly boring in winter.'

'Oh, yes. Frightfully.'

'One misses one's hunting so much.'

'Yes, one does.'

'There's not even much racing to divert one. By the way, I'd plump for Hullabaloo in the Midwinter Handicap at Uttoxeter on Saturday. I lunched with the owner today. It's at a lovely price.'

'Hullabaloo? I'll remember that.'

'I suppose you heard about Associated Metals?' asked the host in a bored voice.

Randolph nodded. 'Yes, of course.'

'Everybody in London seems to know about them,' he complained. 'Still, I'd buy a few before the take-over's made public. One can always do with a little extra cash these overtaxed times.'

'Randolph, *darling*,' announced Debbie, appearing again looking rather pink. 'Time to go.'

'Yes, indeed. Splendid idea.'

'We've got another party.'

'Another?' His face fell.

'Yes, hundreds of miles away in Richmond, or somewhere.'

The party in Richmond was given by an actor in semi-darkness, and before long Debbie was hanging round Randolph's neck biting his ear.

'Here, I say,' he murmured. 'Why don't you and I just sort of…well, push off quietly home?'

'But *darling* we've got *dozens* of parties to go to yet.'

'Oh. Have we?'

'After all, it's Christmas.'

'Yes, I suppose it is.'

'Now don't you worry, my little man.' She patted him again. 'We'll *all* get home in the end.'

They went from Richmond to a rather serious party in a basement at Notting Hill, with people playing the guitar and talking about their souls. The next was a lively affair in Kensington, everyone in false noses and funny hats blowing squeakers. After several more drinks Randolph stopped looking at his watch. After all, it was terrific fun, and for once his evening wasn't going to be ruined by a skeleton in the cupboard.

7

'I'm a trifle worried about my son Randolph,' Mr George Nightrider, MP, was confessing, squashed in Sir Lancelot's bubble car.

'Well, I suppose he's starting to grow up,' returned the surgeon shortly. He didn't like his wife's brother, particularly in the confines of a bubble car.

Mr Nightrider, a tall, saintly-looking man, scratched his long thin nose. 'I should feel happier if he were guarded from the temptations of the turf, the opposite sex, and – er, the second-hand car market. All three seem to hold a heady fascination for him.'

Sir Lancelot turned into Whitehall. 'You can't expect me to keep the feller permanently tied to *my* apron strings. I'm Warden of a College, not a Norland nursemaid.'

'No, of course, I realize you have pressing duties…but… ' Mr Nightrider looked worried. 'Lancelot, may I tell you something in the very deepest confidence?'

'Please do. Though you must excuse me should I not happen to find it particularly interesting.'

'I am to be given Health,' announced Mr Nightrider.

Sir Lancelot raised his eyebrows. 'Delighted to hear it. But I didn't know you'd been ill.'

'I mean the Ministry of Health,' Mr Nightrider corrected him. 'I'm to be shifted from the Ag. and Fish.'

'Good grief,' muttered Sir Lancelot.

'I saw the PM this very morning.' Mr Nightrider looked like a saint with two haloes. 'The announcement is to be made in the New Year. That is why, you understand, the family must be particularly careful not to become tarnished with the slightest breath of scandal. The newspapers... Dear me! The newspapers! I sometimes wonder if a free press is really as necessary as everyone keeps saying. So Randolph must not be involved in any high-spirited student pranks,' he ended severely.

'All right, all right,' grumbled Sir Lancelot, pulling up in Old Palace Yard. 'If you want, I'll tuck him up and kiss him good night.'

The House of Lords, with its flashy Victorian stonework and its fleshy Victorian murals, pleasantly reminds visitors of the Riviera casinos which were put up about the same time. It offers a splendid background for a party, and even Sir Lancelot, after Mr Nightrider had collected their wives from a following taxi, marched up the broad marble staircase inside feeling rather pleased with himself.

Another attraction of the House of Lords is elevating its guests, by two simple labels on the doors, to either Peers or Peeresses. At the top of the marble stairs Paul and Simon were standing outside them, passing the time by chatting.

'The girls must be having a rubber of bridge in there,' nodded Paul.

Simon smiled back. 'It all delays that awful moment when the fellow in hunting pink bellows my name down the hall. It always makes me feel such a prune.'

'Merely a charming natural shyness, my dear chap.' After their competition for the St Swithin's staff, like any men who had fought to the finish an honourable battle, they were on even friendlier terms than before.

Paul tweeked his perfectly tied bow. 'I'm not asking you to tell tales out of school, Simon, but how did the Prof's suggestion go in committee today?'

'Oh, very well. The idea of having a young Warden below consultant status was suddenly thought to be frightfully forward-looking, with it, pop conscious, and all that. They felt the students needed a friend rather than a jailer.'

Paul grinned. 'But if a jailer it's to be, they're lucky to have someone with a flair for the job.'

'The only point worrying me,' frowned Simon, 'is why on earth you want the ruddy appointment anyway? It's a dreadful tie, the pay hardly covers your entertaining, and I should think the house is about as comfortable to live in as the Battersea Dogs' Home.'

'Frankly, I don't. But Deirdre's rather keen on the idea. The Warden, you know, would be a bit of a status symbol for me. If she didn't prod me, I'm far too lazy to push myself up the ladder,' he confessed.

There was a pause, while they greeted a passing bacteriologist from Bart's.

'This really *is* talking out of turn,' Paul resumed awkwardly, 'but I'm wondering if your vote at the election next month is already committed.'

Simon nodded. 'It is.'

'Sir Lancelot, I suppose?'

'No. You.' Simon patted him briefly on the shoulder. 'My dear chap, after a little brush between Sir Lancelot and myself in the theatre last week, I wouldn't vote for him as marker-up of a darts club. And furthermore,' he added grimly, 'I'm so organizing the younger consultants he won't have the chance of a staphylococcus in penicillin of getting the job. Then at least he won't be hanging round our necks in the hospital like a surgical albatross for the rest of his life. Don't thank me, it's pure selfishness,' he added, as Paul started making noises of gratitude. 'I merely want to see the old boy's face when he hears he's been sacked. What *are* those women doing?' he ended, looking at his watch.

'Perhaps it's chess?' suggested Paul.

Unlike men who have fought to the finish an honourable battle, the women who acted as seconds stay frozen in attitudes of icy hatred. They are simply the more logical sex. After all, the most obvious place to stab anyone is in the back, and there's no point in kicking a man unless he's down.

In the Peeresses', Deirdre Ivors-Smith and Nikki Sparrow stood side by side before the mirror touching up their faces.

'But Nikki, darling, that's an absolutely fabulous dress,' cooed Deirdre. 'Where on earth did you find it in London? Or do you pop over to Paris?'

Nikki smoothed her black sheath. 'As a matter of fact, I made it myself.'

'No?' Deirdre was amazed. 'But it looks quite as professional as my Hartnell,' she conceded, indicating her flowing gold and silver skirts. 'Still, I suppose you picked up a good deal of needlework when you were a house-surgeon.' She smiled as she touched a curl of her auburn hair. 'And I expect you've got to lay on the glam a bit now you're moving in such ritzy company.'

Nikki gave a slight frown. 'Oh, you mean tonight?' She laughed. 'I wouldn't call it particularly ritzy. It's mostly the St Swithin's staff cleaned up a bit.'

'But no, dear, I mean Ann Beverley.'

'The film star? I'm afraid we never get nearer to her than the back row of the circle.'

'You're *so* modest, Nikki,' Deirdre complimented her. 'But *I* know your little secret. This very afternoon I noticed Simon and the great lady in the Marlborough – I often drop in there for tea – and I could see they were on terms of the *greatest* chumminess.'

'But I'm afraid you must have made a mistake. Simon hasn't said a word about treating the famous Ann Beverley, and he'd hardly carry professional secrecy to *that* length.'

'Oh, I didn't mean a professional relationship,' declared Deirdre innocently. 'It was obviously a personal one.' She touched Nikki playfully on the chin. 'From what I saw you'll have to look to your laurels. I mean, being kissed by someone like Ann Beverley would turn any man's head,' she threw in gaily. '*And* in public. I was only ten feet away,' she added, to make quite certain. 'Now, we mustn't keep the party waiting a minute longer.'

They left the Peeresses' as Sir Lancelot and Lady Spratt reached the head of the marble staircase with the Nightriders.

'Simon, my boy,' he boomed. 'I would like a little word with you later. About the Warden's election next month.' The senior surgeon slapped him on the back. 'Just to organize our tactics, you know,' he added, with a wink. 'Take my tip, after a lifetime's experience handling committees you should never leave anything to chance.'

'I won't,' Simon assured him.

The man in the red coat bellowed their names, and Sir Lancelot moved towards the high, crowded, tapestry-hung reception hall.

'Sir Lancelot,' said the Duke, who liked to be up in these things. 'I enjoyed your programme on television enormously.'

'That is very kind of Your Grace.'

He took a glass of champagne from a footman in knee-breeches and found himself standing next to Professor Hindehead.

'Ah, Hindehead,' Sir Lancelot greeted him affably. 'Appearing with Bertram Mills' Circus this year?'

'Really, Lancelot!' The Professor's champagne quivered. 'I do wish you'd keep out of my activities. If you want to be a surgical Canute, that's your affair. But I myself believe the modern public wants to be educated.'

'Rubbish, Hindehead,' he snorted. 'They still only want the gory details. They love to see the puke coming up or the baby coming down.'

'It is simply that I wish to humanize the hospital, and I won't have you standing in my way,' snapped the Professor.

Added to the fury over his colleague's surgical ad-libbing on television, the Professor found his scheme for the medical staff wearing name-badges sabotaged that morning by Sir Lancelot prowling the wards behind a large card announcing DR CRIPPEN.

'Bless me, there's the President of the Royal Society,' broke off Sir Lancelot, losing interest. 'Evening, Bongo. We're making a first-class botch-up of it in Australia again, I see. What's your opinion on the wickets they cook up for us out there?'

'The Duke seemed a jovial old card,' observed Simon to his wife, as they squeezed among the crowd. 'Champagne?' he invited, taking a couple of glasses.

'Simon,' asked Nikki, 'do you know Ann Beverley?'

He gave a laugh. 'The film star, you mean?' He took a gulp of champagne. 'As a matter of fact, I was meaning – '

'That stupid woman Deirdre, she absolutely hates me since you got on the staff instead of Paul, just told me some wild story in the loo about you and Ann Beverley embracing in the middle of the Marlborough Hotel. Absolutely fantastic, of course, once you give a second thought to it.'

'Nikki,' Simon began, eyeing the bubbles, 'I think you'd better – '

'Simon, I do want you to meet Dr Longbody, from Manchester,' announced Sir Lancelot, pushing between them. 'He's the world's leading authority on the hookworm. And you, my dear Nikki, must charm this excellent gentleman from Amsterdam, whose name I fear I did not catch.'

'Must be very interesting, the hookworm,' observed Simon, as Sir Lancelot abandoned them.

'It's interesting enough.'

'Much more to a hookworm than meets the eye,' added Simon after a silence.

'I'd say you're right there.'

'Having decent weather up in Manchester?' he went on, as he overheard his wife announcing, 'Oh, I see, you mean you don't speak any English *at all*?'

'Middling,' said Dr Longbody.

'Hasn't been too bad down here.'

'No,' conceded Dr Longbody.

'Dr Clive Moneypenny,' bellowed the man in the red coat, 'and Miss Sowerby.'

Clive strolled in with hands stuck in his pockets and a cigarette dangling from his lips.

'Evening, Professor Hindehead,' he said casually. 'Do you know Miss Sowerby?'

The Professor bowed politely. 'I'm afraid I don't know the name, though I'm sure I'm very familiar with the face.'

'That's very likely. Pat's the barmaid in the King George.'

The Professor straightened up again.

'Good evening,' smiled Pat, who with her red hair and wild silk emerald dress was already attracting the attention of the more prostatic surrounding professors.

'This…this must be quite a treat for you,' muttered the Professor, swallowing.

'Oh, but it is,' returned Pat happily. 'It's the most wonderful outing I've had. Ever since one of the owners took me to the Derby,' she added frankly.

'Why, it's Pat!' exclaimed Paul Ivors-Smith.

'Deirdre, Dr Moneypenny's brought the famous Pat I've told you so much about.'

Deirdre raised her eyebrows. For ten seconds she wondered exactly what to say. 'But what a delicious joke!' she finally decided upon.

'Yes, you always had a keen sense of humour administering a bedpan,' observed Clive mildly.

'My dear Moneypenny – ' Sir Lancelot interrupted forcefully, bursting between them. 'You have certainly risen in my estimation by bringing such a charming young lady to grace our gathering tonight.'

Clive looked surprised, but only shrugged his shoulders. 'It's hardly unusual. One generally takes one's fiancée about socially.'

'Fiancée!' muttered the Professor.

'Didn't you know? We're getting married after Christmas.'

'My dear, I congratulate you most heartily.' Sir Lancelot took Pat's hand. 'Come, let me introduce you to a few people. Possibly you don't know the President of the Royal Society, Moneypenny? Bongo, here a moment, if you please. I want you to meet a couple of friends.'

'Who's that girl, Hindehead?' asked Mr Nightrider, appearing at the Professor's side.

'A barmaid from the public house opposite the hospital,' he explained slowly. 'Brought by that cheeky young man who got his name in the papers.'

'Barmaid? Oh, horror! The Duke, too!'

'Moreover, he is on the point of marrying her.'

'What?' Mr Nightrider looked like a saint slipping into a brand-new hair shirt. 'You can't have scamps like that working in the hospital. I certainly shouldn't have allowed it when I was Chairman of the Governors. I'll have a strong word or two to say next month, believe you me, once I have got the Min…the minute to spare,' he ended quickly. He wiped his brow with his handkerchief. 'Thank merciful heavens even my son in his wildest moments wouldn't get mixed up with a woman bike that.'

His son was at that instant approaching his fourth, and he rather hoped final, party of the evening. The new party seemed in a rum sort of place, but Debbie appeared an enthusiast for quick changes of scene. She handed him a card from her bag. Giggling rather, he passed it to a flunky, who called out his name, getting it quite wrong. He briefly shook hands with his host, and pulled a squeaker from his pocket and blew it. Then he found himself facing his father and Sir Lancelot.

'Oh, obloquy!' cried Mr Nightrider, looking like a saint as they put the torch to the faggots.

'Hello, Dad,' murmured Randolph, standing on one leg.

'Good grief, it's Debbie Dixon,' burst out Sir Lancelot.

'Explain yourself!' hissed Mr Nightrider. 'Explain to me at once exactly what you're doing loose at midnight with the most notorious woman in London?'

Under the influence of mixed drinks since six, Randolph drew himself up. 'Happs to be a lady friend of mine,' he announced haughtily. 'Utterly respectable. Must be. Knows a lot of MPs.' His jaw dropped, as he took another look. 'By golly, so it is,' he added. 'Thought I'd only seen her photo in the society mags.'

'Why there's Lord Worthing,' cried Debbie, diving into the guests. 'Woo-hoo, darling!'

'You are to go to bed instantly,' snapped Mr Nightrider.

Sir Lancelot guffawed loudly at his side. 'That's exactly his idea.'

'Really, Lancelot!' Mr Nightrider rounded. 'This is far from a laughing matter. Return to your rooms at once, Randolph.'

'Yes, Dad.' Randolph turned pale. He felt dreadfully sick as well.

'This matter will be thrashed out in the morning.'

'Yes, Dad.'

'However you found yourself in such company at all is totally beyond my comprehension.'

'Yes, Dad.'

'Come on, I'll give you a lift in my bubble car,' offered Sir Lancelot. 'I'm getting bored here, anyway. You shouldn't worry about the lad,' he added, digging his brother-in-law hard in the ribs. 'It's extremely unlikely a St Swithin's medical student could ever afford the ante.'

'I am ruined!' muttered Mr Nightrider, covering his white face with his hands. 'Utterly and irrevocably ruined.'

'Sorry about that, George,' returned Sir Lancelot amiably, 'but *I've* had the best laugh of the year. Come along, young man. If I were you I should let the attendant take your squeaker.'

'Yes, the hookworm,' Dr Longbody was saying to Simon, as the pair brushed past, 'is an absolutely fascinating little beast. When you get to know him, of course.'

Simon noticed Nikki talking to Deirdre. He really ought to put her straight about Ann Beverley.

8

'Good morning, Mr Sparrow,' said Miss Scutts brightly at nine the following morning in Harley Street. 'You have an early visitor.'

'Just my luck,' grumbled Simon, 'this particular morning.'

The hookworm expert from Manchester had turned out terribly amusing in the end, and they had stayed far too long at the reception. Apart from a shocking hangover, his mind was confused about the Ann Beverley nonsense. He had intended to put the facts to Nikki, but someone always seemed to interrupt at the party, last night he'd been too tired, and early that morning he'd been too rushed.

The clever psychiatrists, of course, would say he was simply suppressing the information through subconscious feelings of guilt. And perhaps the clever psychiatrists would be right. He had decided, driving to Harley Street, the whole affair was so utterly trivial, he would never set eyes on the actress again, and raising the topic would cause only unnecessary complications. What was the point, he asked himself reasonably, when Nikki seemed to believe him innocent anyway?

'Who sent the patient?' Simon added, slipping off his coat. 'Dr Dinwiddie?'

'It isn't a patient, Mr Sparrow. It's Dr Defoe.'

'Defoe?'

'Dr Angus Defoe, from across the way.'

'Good lord,' muttered Simon. 'So he comes for proper treatment himself while submitting his victims to twentieth-century witchcraft? Well, I can't see the fellow till I've collected myself. I'll give you a buzz to show him up.'

There was only one letter on his consulting desk upstairs. It was from his bank manager, to whom he had written from the Harley Street address in the hope of making an impression. He hadn't. He slipped it in his pocket and touched the buzzer.

'Good morning, Mr Defoe,' began Simon, holding out a hand but preserving the proprieties of prefixes.

'Good morning. So this is Mr Sparrow? Well, now. And we are neighbours.'

'We share the same parking meter,' nodded Simon briefly. 'Won't you sit down?'

'Thank you.'

Dr Defoe had wavy brown hair and the craggily mature good looks of the men in the cornflake advertisements. His blue suit was neat, but might have been admired more in Charing Cross Road than Savile Row. He had a flower in his buttonhole, suede ankle boots, a thickly striped shirt, heavy gold cuff-links, a gold tie-clip, a gold watch on one wrist, and a gold identity bracelet on the other. He made Simon feel as square as a ship's biscuit.

'And what can I do for you?' asked Simon.

'Write me a cheque for ten thousand pounds.'

Simon raised an eyebrow.

'Well, yes. But after that?'

'Mr Sparrow – ' He put together his carefully maintained fingertips. 'As you may be aware, I am a Doctor of the Institute of Vibrology, which is centred in the United States. In Tuscaloosa,' he added briefly. 'I am not a medical man, which admittedly allows me a certain freedom of practice. Though I confess with some envy the lack of a medical diploma leaves me occasionally at a serious disadvantage. For example, I have not the protection of an elaborate apparatus of professional ethics.'

'I do wish you'd come to the point,' cut in Simon crossly.

'But I have already reached it, Mr Sparrow. With the ten thousand pounds. That is what you must pay me in settlement of my claim.'

Simon rose. 'Thank you, Mr Defoe, for calling. But I can't see any point in carrying this facetious conversation any further. I have a roomful of patients waiting to see me downstairs.'

'Not so fast, my friend.' Dr Defoe caught him with a cold eye. 'Had I been a medical practitioner, you would have found yourself in the most serious trouble with the General Medical Council for running down my professional abilities to my patient – an extremely valued patient, for whom I have done an enormous amount of good, if you will permit my lapse of modesty. Luckily,' he continued, rearranging his suede boots, 'as a simple British subject I still enjoy the protection of the courts, who will undoubtedly award a man of my position the heaviest damages for slander. A rogue, Mr Sparrow?' he enquired amiably. 'A charlatan? A danger to the public? A therapist with the eye of newt and tongue of frog? I've already seen my solicitor, and he tells me you haven't a hope,' he added in a more informative tone.

Simon drew a breath. 'Well, you *are* a rogue. You are a charlatan. And in my opinion you're the greatest danger to the public since Jack the Ripper went out of business.'

'If only we had a witness!' complained Dr Defoe wearily. 'Then it would be fifteen thousand. Oh, I understand your feelings, Mr Sparrow. I understand them perfectly. There are many methods of healing in this world, and unhappily you medical people rather uncharitably recognize only one of them.'

'Look here, Defoe – ' Simon stabbed a finger. 'I know damn well that little green case of yours is nothing but a bag of rubbish. And so does everyone else who understands the first thing about it. Terrestrial vibrations, indeed! You might just as well make incantations over the patient's nail clippings.'

'You try my patience, Mr Sparrow. But I will strain my sympathy to see your point of view. However, you could never sustain it in court. I can bring countless patients, some of them extremely eminent, to swear the benefit I have brought them. Now look here, young feller me lad,' he added more briskly, getting up. 'Ten thousand, or you're in trouble. Go to court and you'll have your costs to find as well.'

'How the hell do you imagine I can get hold of ten thousand pounds?' Simon demanded angrily.

'Oh, I'm not pressing. I'm perfectly reasonable. To a fault. I'll give you till New Year's day. A whole fortnight. You can't say I'm not generous, can you?'

'Get out, you nasty piece of sewage.'

Dr Defoe compressed his thin lips. 'I'm afraid I don't stoop to abuse,' he explained. 'In a fortnight's time I shall expect you to step across the street and pay a call.' The lips twisted into a smile. 'A sort of first footing you might say? Good morning.'

He left Simon gripping the edge of the desk.

'Is anything the matter?' asked Miss Scutts anxiously from the door.

'Eh? No, just a…a difficult consultation, that's all.' He bit his thumb. 'Ring up the Marlborough Hotel, will you? Ask when I can see Miss Beverley for a few minutes.'

He paced up and down the consulting room.

'Ten thousand quid!' he muttered. 'But it's fantastic! Surely no court in the world… ' He shrugged his shoulders. 'What a bloody fool I am!' he agreed with himself heartily.

'Miss Beverley's away at the studio till midday,' announced Miss Scutts. 'But she'd be happy to see you then.'

'All right,' Simon nodded. 'By the way, have you got any aspirin down there?'

Aspirin was simultaneously being swallowed by Randolph Nightrider in his room at the College. It was his sixth of the morning. At even his early stage of study he'd heard of salicylate poisoning, but he didn't care. It was the most awful morning of his life. He had already resignedly packed his trunk, boxed up his books, and disarticulated his skeleton. He only awaited the awful summons to Sir Lancelot's presence. He felt death would be rather an anti-climax.

After half an hour sitting on the trunk chewing his nails, he decided to get the execution of his career over as speedily as possible. Squaring his shoulders, he marched along the corridor. He descended the stairs, his spirits sinking with each step. He opened the door to the adjoining Warden's Lodge with a fluttering feeling in the knees, and finally achieved a timid tap on the big oak door.

'Enter.'

Sir Lancelot was sitting in an armchair by the fireplace, reading the Bible.

'Yes?'

'You – er, wanted to see me, sir,' said Randolph.

Sir Lancelot considered. 'No, I don't think so.'

Randolph blinked. 'But surely, sir my – er, conduct.'

'Oh, yes.' Sir Lancelot laid the book aside. 'Mrs Chuffey reports there are two cigarette burns on your dressing-table. If you must indulge in the habit of smoking cigarettes, please confine the damage to your own lungs. Good morning.'

'But last night, sir!' he cried.

'My dear fellow, last night is no concern of mine. If you wish to hobnob with ladies of light virtue in your spare time, you are entitled to as much as any other citizen. As long as you don't tackle them in the College, of course.'

'You…you mean I can stay in the hospital?' exclaimed Randolph, a suggestion of the normal strawberry suffusing his blancmange-like face.

'I should indeed like to know why you are not in your anatomy lecture this very moment. Your father has been on the telephone a few times this morning,' Sir Lancelot mentioned as an afterthought.

' 'Fraid the Old Man might be a bit cut up,' Randolph perceived.

The Warden nodded. 'He seems to think he should emigrate permanently to the Chiltern Hundreds. Doubtless the mood will pass. By the way – ' Sir Lancelot produced his wallet. 'The bank cleared that cheque for the Rolls. Here's my own for your commission. Five hundred pounds.'

'Urk,' said Randolph, taking it.

'I would only advise you, my boy, not to spend it on Debbie Dixon. I fancy she is a one-way street to ruin.'

'Not on your life, sir,' Randolph told him warmly. 'Every penny will be put to good use, sir.'

'Why, hello, Randolph,' said Lady Spratt, coming in. 'Are you sure you're quite well? You're always looking so poorly these days.'

'Are you familiar with the Scriptures?' Sir Lancelot added in Randolph's direction.

'Got the Divinity prize at school, actually.'

'Good. Then you can read the student's lesson in the carol service tonight. The Chaplain has very kindly invited me to give the final one.'

Near every Christmas the hospital pleasantly observed the service of the Nine Carols in the Chapel, with the lessons read by probationer, student, staff nurse, houseman, sister, registrar, junior consultant, house governor, and a senior consultant as the climax. The Chaplain had not, in fact, invited Sir Lancelot at all, but for many Christmases now he had simply risen from his pew and intoned the last lesson as a matter of course.

'Absolutely delighted, sir.' Randolph threw a glance at Lady Spratt. 'And believe me, sir, I'll never so much as look at a…a you-know-what again as long as I live.'

'You really ought to put some sedative in that boy's tea in the morning,' muttered Sir Lancelot, as Randolph shut the door and ran straight into Susan Grantchester.

'Oh, hello,' he said brightly.

'Hello, Randolph! Didn't see you at breakfast.'

'Bit bilious.' He tapped his abdomen. 'Something I ate yesterday.'

'But you poor boy.' Her tender look was ointment to his bruised soul. 'Don't you think you should go across to Cas. and get some antacid?'

'Be all right soon,' he declared bravely. 'How's the lip?'

'They've given a student called Forcedyke your part.'

'Oh, Filthy Fred. H'm.'

Susan dropped her eyes. 'I wish it were you, Randolph.'

'I say, do you?' He couldn't imagine how on earth he'd succumbed to Debbie Dixon. 'I won't be far away, you know, looking after the props. Jolly responsible job, the props.'

'I'm sure I shan't get stage fright at all,' she breathed, 'feeling you're so near.'

'You know, that's terribly – Shall we get across to the dissecting room?' he added hastily, as the door opened and Sir Lancelot began to emerge.

'Don't forget the jumble sale this afternoon, Lancelot,' came from behind him.

'That rag-fight! Yet another imposition of what is laughingly called the festive season. What's for lunch in Hall?' he asked over his shoulder.

'Macaroni cheese,' said Lady Spratt.

'Thank heavens I'm lunching out. The hostess may not be exactly my choice, but at least the grub should be good.'

His hostess was at that moment having words with his host.

'Why on earth did you have to ask that couple on the spur of the moment?' complained Deirdre Ivors-Smith, stubbing out her cigarette in the Italian ashtray and flopping back on the Swedish sofa in the elegant little drawing-room of their charming little house in one of the most fashionable of Chelsea squares. 'I though we saw quite enough of them last night.'

'But why not?' Paul shrugged his shoulders. 'After all, Clive Moneypenny is a colleague, and a perfectly decent sort. Though possibly inclined to be rather bitter.'

'Bitter!' muttered Deirdre, who hadn't forgotten the bedpans.

'Anyway, he's an Old Etonian,' Paul justified it all.

'But what about that awful female?'

'Pat's a perfect lady,' countered her husband warmly. 'Surely you noticed last night, she has absolutely natural charm and dignity? Towards everyone, including the Duke?'

'Yes, I suppose serving behind a bar gives you the knack,' admitted Deirdre.

'Darling, you mustn't be a snob.'

'Snob? Me a snob? Don't be ridiculous. It's only that you've upset my plan for the table.'

'Well, you don't have to cook the ruddy lunch.' Paul reached for the *British Medical Journal*. 'Though I must say, I don't know why you're having the party at all. I see quite enough of Sir Lancelot at St Swithin's.'

'I'm only doing my best for you, my dear. You told me yourself how Dr Knickerbocker was such an important American surgeon. Either he or Dr Burton might get you a good job in the States.'

'But I don't *want* a job in the States,' sighed Paul over his *Journal*. 'There's no cricket or draught beer.'

'Sometimes, darling, I think you can be really quite selfish,' declared Deirdre, reaching for another cigarette.

The morning after the reception was not a happy one for the St Swithin's contingent, but none explored the substratum of misery suffered by Simon Sparrow. He hurried into the Marlborough Hotel at noon with thoughts of selling his home and car, cancelling his son's place at school, resigning, emigrating, and starting all over again in the Australian outback. Worse still, it occurred to him, how the devil was he going to explain it to Nikki now?

'Miss Beverley, please,' he asked the girl at the reception desk. 'I have an appointment.'

'Mr Sparrow?' She reached for a telephone. 'Would you like to go up?'

'I'd rather she came down here.'

'My, what's the matter?' asked Ann Beverley, when she appeared from the lift. 'You look as though you've seen all the ghosts in Shakespeare.'

'Miss Beverley – I've got to speak to you urgently.'

'Sure.' She took a puff from her gold holder. 'Can we do it over a drink?'

Finding a corner of the bar, Simon described in crushed undertones his visit from across the street.

'Gee, but I never thought… ' The actress twisted her martini glass anxiously. 'I guess I got so steamed up over all you said, when Defoe bounced in last night with his little green case I blew my top.'

Simon gave a sigh. 'I'm afraid it all adds up to a neat diagnosis of slander, however you look at it.'

'Am I sorry! Do you suppose it would do if I called him and explained I'd made the whole story up? Hysterical film star has outburst, temperament, and that?'

'It's a kind thought, but I'm afraid it's too late.'

She took another puff from her holder. 'How about the old charm? He might come across with enough of it.'

'That's an even kinder thought, but with cash in the offing he'd be about as susceptible as Nelson in Trafalgar Square.'

'I guess you're right. Aw, hell! What a hole I've got you in.' She thought a moment. 'Say, how about calling my London lawyers and asking what they can do? See here – ' She scribbled with Simon's pencil on a cocktail coaster. 'Dwye, Evans and Pick, of Furnival's Inn. And boy, there're less flies on that set-up than on the polar ice-cap. I'll write them to charge it to me.'

'That's terribly good of you,' mumbled Simon, grasping the coaster like a drowning man his straw. 'I'll go back to Harley Street to ring them at once, and hope they can see me this afternoon.'

'And it happened to the nicest guy,' sighed Ann Beverley, as they finished their drinks and strolled thoughtfully through the hall to the front door. 'Well, so long, honey,' she ended on the steps. 'You let me know what those legal boys of mine cook up, won't you?'

Simon was so distracted he hardly noticed she'd kissed him again. He turned round to find himself facing Paul and Deirdre Ivors-Smith, Sir Lancelot Spratt, Clive Moneypenny with Pat, and a fat man and thin one all arriving for their lunch.

'Oh, God!' he cried, covering his mouth with a hand.

'Friends of yours?' asked Ann Beverley lightly. 'He's sweet,' she smiled at them, disappearing inside.

'That…that was Ann Beverley,' Simon blurted out in explanation.

'Our Ann sure gets friendly with the natives,' observed the thin man with a laugh.

'Oh, no, she only happens to be one of my patients,' Simon found himself adding hurriedly. 'I mean – '

'Well!' Deirdre exclaimed, all over again.

'Good show!' grinned Paul.

'I sometimes wonder,' observed Sir Lancelot Spratt, 'if I am getting sadly out of touch with the clinical technique in the younger section of the profession. Shall we get out of the cold?'

But Simon had already burst through them and stumbled somehow towards his car.

9

Our kindest social convention dictates that any really first-class clanger, though keenly observed by everybody at the time, is never commented upon afterwards, nor even assumed to have happened. Apart from Sir Lancelot Spratt mumbling something obscure about Simon Sparrow and Randolph Nightrider being in the same dreamboat, no one mentioned the touching little scene on the steps. Besides, they were all looking forward to a Marlborough Hotel lunch.

'Would Dr Knickerbocker sit on Sir Lancelot's right,' Deirdre directed the fat American, 'and Dr Burton on his left,' she organized the thin one. 'Clive, I'm afraid I must separate you from your charming fiancée, but I too must suffer separation from Paul.'

We have perhaps not seen Deirdre Ivors-Smith at her best. She was a conscientious and pleasing hostess, and if over-ambitious for her husband to rise in the profession she once shared herself, there was nothing else to jog the clever, lazy, well-off man into bettering his surgical status. Though perhaps the warmth of her charm that morning reflected her glowing anticipation of telling Nikki Sparrow about Simon's repeat performance – right after lunch at the hospital jumble sale.

'What will you have to drink, Dr Knickerbocker?' Deirdre invited as the waiter approached.

'Coca-Cola, thank you. I never touch alcohol,' asserted the fat surgeon.

'And Dr Burton?'

'Oh, Scotch and soda. I never touch Coca-Cola,'

'How about you, Pat?' Deirdre gave a little laugh. 'Though I'm afraid you must know very much more about the subject than me.'

Sir Lancelot glared at his hostess. Clive was lolling back in his chair apparently absorbing the menu.

'I guess you're eager to hear my technique of organ transplantation,' Dr Knickerbocker rolled across the table.

'Naturally,' murmured Sir Lancelot, already wishing he had settled for the macaroni cheese.

'They have some excellent oysters,' announced Paul.

'No thank you.' Dr Knickerbocker held up a hand. 'Oysters disagree with me.'

'They disagree with me, too,' nodded Dr Burton. 'May I have a dozen?'

Dr Knickerbocker pitched into his organ transplantation.

He shifted lungs with the sole *bonne femme*, kidneys with the *boeuf Strogonoff*, hearts with the ice-cream, and pieces of liver with his Scotch woodcock. He lasted, with interruptions from Sir Lancelot trying to change the subject, until the coffee.

'And what is your interest in medicine, Dr Moneypenny?' he enquired, taking notice of the company as he tidied the last transplanted organ into place.

'Neuromuscular physiology,' explained Clive briefly. 'I've spent three years finding out what makes a muscle contract.'

Dr Knickerbocker nodded gravely. 'And what practical application has that, may I ask?'

'None whatsoever.'

'This very charming young lady you're going to marry,' cut in Dr Burton. 'Is she connected with medicine as well?'

'Oh, no,' nodded Clive. 'Pat's a barmaid.'

Dr Knickerbocker gave a grunt, as though finding alcohol in his Coca-Cola.

'You don't say?' smiled Dr Burton. 'That's nice.'

'I feel I'm almost part of the hospital, I must admit,' Pat smiled back, not seeming to find anything amiss in the conversation. 'I work in the pub opposite St Swithin's, you see. I think I see more doctors than the patients put together.'

'You ought to be expelled from the hospital, Moneypenny,' grunted Sir Lancelot, swirling his brandy round the glass. Deirdre looked up quickly. 'For taking the company of this delightful girl away from us,' he added.

'I expect your family must be very pleased, Pat,' Deirdre added sharply. 'I mean, your marrying a doctor.'

'Of course,' agreed Pat. 'So were yours, weren't they?'

'Cold for the time of year,' observed Sir Lancelot.

Deirdre drew a breath. Clive was studying his cigar. Paul gathered up the shattered conversation and threw it back on the table remarking, 'I believe you were kindly considering me for a post in your clinic, Dr Knickerbocker?'

'That is so,' rolled out of him. 'Maybe around Easter.'

'I'd like to think out the pros and cons, if I may,' Paul added. 'There are – er, certain events occurring in the summer which make me hesitant to leave.'

'Yes, the West Indians are touring next season,' Sir Lancelot nodded in agreement.

'How about you, Dr Moneypenny?' rumbled Dr Knickerbocker. 'Are you likely to be working in the United States?'

'Not very.' Clive tossed aside his napkin. 'You see, I'm a Communist.

'A what?'

Dr Knickerbocker rose several inches. If somebody had substituted for Clive a bad case of leprosy he wouldn't have looked more alarmed.

'Well, that's original, at any rate,' observed Dr Burton lightly.

'You mean…' Dr Knickerbocker's brows gathered in mighty knots. 'You're a card-carrying party member?'

'I rather fancy I've mislaid the card.' Clive scratched his ear. 'As a matter of fact, I wasn't a member for very long.'

'But you're still a Commie at heart?' persisted Dr Knickerbocker in senatorial tones.

'*I* used to know Harry Pollitt very well,' mentioned Sir Lancelot.

'I haven't really thought about it for some time,' confessed Clive. 'But I'm either a Communist or a Liberal. I have a psychological fetish for minorities.'

'I guess it's time for my next appointment,' announced Dr Knickerbocker.

The party broke up. Dr Knickerbocker shook hands with Paul Ivors-Smith extremely gingerly. You never knew how this contagion spread.

'You intrigue me,' condescended Clive, as Sir Lancelot hustled him and Pat into a taxi.

'St Swithin's Hospital, driver. Indeed?'

'Last night you went to enormous trouble introducing Pat to the nobs.' Clive lounged back in the seat. 'And today, when the world's sweetheart started operations, you rushed to her defence with clank of armour and flash of steel.'

'Perhaps it is simply that I admire your choice,' returned Sir Lancelot briefly, 'in more senses than one.'

'If Pat had spent six months learning to work a typewriter, nobody would even think twice about her job.'

'Snobbishness and pettiness,' snorted Sir Lancelot. 'Our national vice. It's already lost us an Empire.'

'And I always imagined you the biggest surgical blimp ever to chortle at the sight of blood,' added Clive amiably.

'H'm,' said Sir Lancelot, tugging his beard.

'Anyway, the whole thing's so utterly trivial, isn't it, darling? What the hell does it matter if you happen to work in a pub? You don't care a damn what that paranoid vampire Deirdre says about you, do you?'

'Not a scrap,' asserted Pat vigorously.

Clive patted her hand. 'I know you don't lose any sleep over it.'

'Not a wink,' Pat nodded energetically.

'That attitude of accepting you on sufferance – it's pitiable, really.'

'Yes, ever so pitiable,' declared Pat stoutly, and burst into tears.

'Driver!' Sir Lancelot hammered on the partition with his umbrella. 'Let me off! I intend to finish my journey by bus.'

'It's no good.' Pat snuggled against Clive's lapel as Sir Lancelot jumped among the Piccadilly traffic. 'It's a mad idea our getting married. It's crazy.'

Clive regarded her as he would inspect a muscle which had reacted abnormally to electrical stimulus. Though entranced by the same charms as drew other customers into the King George, he was particularly attracted by Pat being such a sensible level-headed female organism. And now the woman was behaving like an idiot.

'Of course it isn't crazy,' he said shortly.

'I'd just hold up your career – '

'Career? What career? I shall go on messing about in the basement of St Swithin's until I'm senile enough to claim on the Medical Benevolent Fund, as far as I can make out.'

'Clive darling…you know that Colonel said you had brilliant prospects.'

'Colonel?' He frowned. 'Oh, at the House of Lords? The fellow who got me invited? He was probably drunk. Those Army doctors always are.' He tugged his ear. He was as severely allergic to emotional scenes as Sir Lancelot. 'Look, Pat – we must think about the whole affair calmly and intelligently. Till Christmas, at any rate. Honestly, darling, I don't know what I'd do without you.'

'There's dozens of nice girls in the hospital who could look after you better than me.'

'Now you make me sound like a chronic case of something peculiar.' He stared at his reflection in the driver's glass partition. 'Perhaps I am,' he admitted.

Deirdre drove Paul's Lagonda to the hospital. She parked it in the courtyard and made for Founders' Hall and the jumble sale in an excellent mood. The lunch had admittedly not been much of a success, and that stupid Moneypenny man had probably sunk Paul's chances of ever getting a job in America at all. But now she really had something to tell Nikki Sparrow.

'Why, Nikki my dear,' she began, advancing on a stall in the corner. 'Lovely to see you. How's trade?'

'Hello, Deirdre,' Nikki smiled back. 'Like the first day of Harrod's sale. It's a thing for taking off riding boots,' she explained to a customer. 'Terribly useful, you see. If of course you happen to have any riding boots.'

'I thought last night Simon said he was coming to help? Which is more than Paul would rise to, I must say.'

'I had a phone call to say he was held up on a case. Yes, madam, the gramophone works wonderfully. You wind it up, you see. So handy in case the electricity fails.'

'His practice seems to be flourishing,' observed Deirdre admiringly. 'Shall I help instead?'

'I'd love you to. Yes, it's a book of family photos. I'm afraid I don't know who the family are, but they look very charming people.'

'We've just had a nice little lunch in the Marlborough,' Deirdre continued, moving carefully into the kill. 'Just Sir Lancelot and two charming Americans. And Clive with his fiancée, of course. One feels one must do something for them socially.'

Nikki nodded. 'Mah-jong,' she explained across the counter. 'A terribly interesting game. Some of the pieces are missing, but I'm sure there's quite enough to play with just the same.'

'Doesn't Simon ever take you to the Marlborough?' Deirdre enquired, shifting a large piece of china with CORONATION OF KING EDWARD THE EIGHTH written on it.

'I'm afraid the practice will have to flourish rather more first.'

'But he's *always* taking Ann Beverley there.'

Nikki turned her head. 'Deirdre, I do wish you wouldn't go on about Ann Beverley. Simon would have told me if there'd been a scrap of truth in it.'

Deirdre's eyes widened. 'But Nikki, I saw him there again this very lunchtime. *And* kissing her on the front steps. He's making quite a habit of it.'

'Really, I – it's a billiard cue, and tip's come off – I'm afraid I just damn well don't believe you.'

'I'm sorry.' Deirdre looked hurt. 'But if you think I'm telling lies, you'd better ask Sir Lancelot, not to mention the Moneypenny couple. They saw him too.'

Nikki frowned.

'Not that I can blame Simon,' Deirdre smiled. 'She looks so lovely, just as she does on the films. And so sexy as well. Here comes Simon now,' she announced brightly, glancing down the hall. 'Then I'll be off. You won't need me with him to help you, will you?'

Simon stumbled through the hall, hardly noticing the jovial transactions going on all round. He'd hoped his visit to Dwye, Evans and Pick would relieve his black despair with brilliant shafts of legal sunlight. Instead, they'd only added to the miserable condition a cold drizzle of pessimism.

'He's asking ten thousand pounds, Mr Sparrow?' demanded Mr Pick, a short, cheerful bald man whose legal black coat and legal white shirt gave the air of an amiable penguin. 'It's rubbish. Utter rubbish!'

'Am I relieved to hear that,' murmured Simon across the desk.

'You mean he actually had the cheek to walk into your consulting rooms and demand it? Ten thousand pounds! I don't know what public morality is coming to.'

'It's hardly fair to the public, burdening them with Defoe's morals.'

'Ten thousand pounds!' repeated Mr Pick warmly. 'Five thousand I'd say was nearer the mark.'

Simon looked up. 'You mean he's got…well, a sort of case?'

'Oh, there's no doubt of that,' explained Mr Pick affably. 'Though I expect you can settle for five thousand very easily.'

'But I haven't got five thousand pounds!' cried Simon.

'Ah, well,' said Mr Pick.

'Simon,' announced Nikki as he reached her stall, 'have you been making love to Ann Beverley?'

'Ann Beverley?' In the stress of the afternoon, even his public performance at lunchtime had slipped from his mind. 'Oh, Ann Beverley. As a matter of fact, I can explain everything.'

'Please do,' said Nikki crisply, looking straight ahead. 'It's called a washboard, madam. You can do your laundry on it if the washing machine breaks down. Yes, Simon?'

'I mean, the whole thing was perfectly innocent from beginning to end. Both times.'

'Oh? So you *were* necking with her on the front steps of the Marlborough yesterday as well?'

'Nikki! I must ask you to believe – '

'You led me to believe you weren't last night. Rather chancing your arm, isn't it, trying the same tactics again?'

'But darling! I assure you I hadn't the slightest – '

'Ah, our handsome married couple!' beamed the hospital chaplain across the junk. 'How nice to see you both co-operating in this splendid venture! I wish some of the other consultants and their ladies would do the same.'

'Thank you very much,' said Nikki briskly.

'I always say the staff of a hospital is a family,' continued the chaplain, who said so very often indeed. 'We have our little trials but our many joys together, and we are always fortified to know our colleagues stand ready to help us with the same charity of our own family circle. What better festival for the family than Christmas – '

'I'm sure you have a lot of other stalls to visit, Padre,' muttered Simon.

'You will be reading the junior consultant's lesson tonight as arranged, I hope?'

'Oh! Yes. Of course. Thank you for reminding me.'

'Six o'clock, then. I won't intrude any longer. What a sturdy-looking flat-iron! I'm sure some home can find excellent use for it.'

'What the hell's wrong with being kissed a couple of times in broad daylight by a famous film star, anyway?' countered Simon. 'It's something to be rather proud of, I'd say.'

'Have you or have you not been making me look an utter fool to that woman Deirdre? And giving me a packet of lies?' demanded Nikki. 'Jumbo size,' she added.

'Yes,' said Simon.

'Good afternoon,' said Nikki, stalking off.

'But Nikki – ! I don't know what the devil it is, my dear sir, but it looks like a second-hand lavatory brush – Nikki – !'

'Ah, Simon,' began Sir Lancelot Spratt, propping his stomach over the goods. 'I don't know what you were up to today, but if you keep your nose clean with the General Medical Council, I suppose it's your affair. I would just like a word with you about this rather tedious election business for the Wardenship. As you know, Cambridge and his excellent colleagues are behind me, quite as solidly as the Professor's nasty little clique is against. I'd just like to give your marching orders for organizing an absolutely thumping majority. It so happens I particularly wish to beat young Ivors-Smith hands down – nothing personal, to be sure – in fact I have just enjoyed a very good lunch – '

'I have no intention whatever of voting for you, you great burbling bladder of bull,' snapped Simon. 'I have already done my canvassing thank you very much, and the junior consultants needed no persuasion whatever in promising their votes for old Paul. And furthermore, Sir Lancelot, when the result comes out I shall throw up my hat and dance a wild fandango right in the middle of the courtyard. It's an umbrella, you bloody fool,' he shouted to the next customer. 'And it's got holes in it.'

He stalked off, too.

So we find everyone approaching the season of goodwill wallowing in bad-tempered frustration. Arriving at St Swithin's that afternoon, Paul Ivors-Smith found his ward sister in a thunderous mood, a pile of National Health forms to sign, and a note from the hospital accountant about his income tax, and suddenly decided it would have been a great idea to live in America after all. Randolph Nightrider, his heart spring-cleaned and vacant for the new occupant, sat biting his finger-nails at a rehearsal in the common room while Susan enthusiastically threw herself into the arms of Filthy Fred. His diversion into the arms of Debbie Dixon had left him far behind in the hot-run race. Clive Moneypenny reached the Shangri-La wondering whether to be angry with himself and worried about Pat or vice versa.

'Why, what's the matter, Dr Moneypenny?' exclaimed the pretty waitress, who was dusting the hall with its worn lino and greasy walls haunted by a legion of dead dinners. 'You look as though you've gone and lost your soul.'

'I may well have this afternoon, in a taxi in Piccadilly,' he replied bleakly. The horrifying possibility of life without Pat had only just occurred to him. 'Fenella,' he asked suddenly, 'have you ever heard of the Nobel Prize?'

She smiled. 'That would be a horse race?'

'More like a sweepstake. How would *you* like to marry a doctor and go to the beautiful city of Stockholm and shake hands with the King and sit in a wonderful dress while the greatest scientists in the world came to congratulate your husband with faintly-disguised envy? There'd be lovely snacks, too. The Swedes are awfully good at that sort of thing.'

"Well, now, that would depend a lot on the doctor, wouldn't it?'

He nodded sadly. 'I suppose Pat thinks I'm not worth the effort.'

'Will you please let that girl get on with her work,' snapped Mrs Brewis appearing downstairs. 'She's behind enough as it is.'

'By the way, I shan't be in for supper,' Clive told his landlady casually, 'I'm going to church.'

It was the only time in the year he did. It satisfied his aestheticism if not his atheism. And that Christmas, the Victorian chapel by the main gate of St Swithin's had never looked prettier. The chaplain's wife had made a better show than ever before with the decorations, the holly-decked lights gleamed softly on the rows of nurses, with their scarlet and black corridor capes and their starched caps turning up at the back like the tails of perching doves. The chaplain was in excellent voice, and everyone joined in the carols.

Only in the lesson reader's pew was the spirit of the occasion regrettably lacking. While Randolph Nightrider stood at the lectern on one leg, Simon and Sir Lancelot sat wedged against each other harbouring their differing bleak thoughts. Simon reflected it would be his last Christmas with a job, and probably with a wife, and wondered if he dare even go home for dinner. Sir Lancelot was trying to make up his mind whether to be bitterly sad or flamingly furious at Simon's black ingratitude. 'To think,' he muttered to himself, with highly unchristian sideway glances, 'of all I've done for him!'

When Simon's turn came he kept losing his place, and everyone agreed Sir Lancelot did not mouth his verses as majestically as usual. The senior surgeon returned and sat slumped in his corner while the Chaplain gave a short address, on the staff of a hospital being like a family.

'Family!' muttered Sir Lancelot bleakly. He stroked his beard. 'Family?' he asked himself. He thought deeply for some moments. 'The family…? By George!' He sat up in his pew. 'The family ! – That's it!'

They rose for the final carol, and Sir Lancelot put a five-pound note in the collection.

Without a word he strode from the chapel across the courtyard. He jumped up the steps of the library.

'Miggs!' he shouted. 'Miggs! Where are you, man! Miggs!'

'I was just going off home, Sir Lancelot,' announced the little librarian apologetically, trying to hide round a bookcase.

'You're not. Get me the Hospital Charter – the original one, from Henry the Eighth. Also every damn document about the College you can lay your hands on.'

'Yes, of course, Sir Lancelot.' Miggs looked up at him anxiously. 'But wouldn't the morning do? After all, it is getting on for Christmas – '

'The morning will *not* do. Furthermore, a dozen Glenlivet malt whisky will arrive on your doorstep tomorrow with my compliments.'

'Oh, Sir Lancelot! Thank you – '

'Don't burble, man, get on with it. Lights! Put on some lights! I've got hard work to do.'

At three in the morning one of the housemen making for bed after a perforation noticed the library windows ablaze. Peeping through, he saw Sir Lancelot scribbling furiously amid a pile of books.

'Oh, well,' observed the houseman, yawning and shutting the door. 'I suppose that's one way of doing your football pools.'

When Sir Lancelot decided to upset an apple cart, he never left much intact but the pips.

10

Christmas Eve started as one of those cold, grey, uncertain sort of English winter days, when the sky might be full of snow, sleet, hail, or rain, but whatever it is seems likely to drop on you at any moment. Sir Lancelot Spratt, stepping briskly across the road to the hospital after breakfast, made his way through Out Patients' to the almoner's office radiating midsummer sunshine.

'Good morning, Mrs Armitage,' he boomed to the pleasant-looking woman behind the desk. 'You have acquired a young lady for me, I hope?'

'Oh, good morning, Sir Lancelot.' The Almoner smiled back. 'Yes, she's playing happily in the crèche at this moment.' She pressed a button. 'It was very generous of you, Sir Lancelot, to participate in the Child for Christmas scheme personally.'

'One must express the spirit of the season,' he explained grandly. 'The girl is, I trust, quite clean?'

'Oh, yes, Sir Lancelot!'

'No flits, impetigo, measles, scabies, and all that sort of thing?'

'I assure you she comes from a perfectly sanitary home. It's simply that her father must be away on business a good deal, and the domestic atmosphere doesn't seem very satisfactory.'

'Honest, I hope?' he added. 'These days they seem to start burglary from the cradle.'

'Of course she's honest, Sir Lancelot,' returned the Almoner, more briefly.

'Quiet in her demeanour, I trust? Respectful? I cannot stand uppish children. Obedient? And her table manners? I expect the rudiments, as I have to eat my own Christmas dinner watching them.'

'You will find Marylin Shufflewell an extremely polite, honest, shy, well-mannered little girl,' the Almoner told him rather wearily, as a nurse brought in a dark-haired large-eyed child of about six in a green velvet dress.

'Well, Marylin, are you looking forward to Christmas?' Sir Lancelot began heartily.

'Yes, thank you.'

'You won't miss your own daddy?'

'No, thank you.'

'Do you wash your face and say your prayers before going to bed?'

'Yes, thank you.'

'You're not frightened of me, are you?'

'No, thank you.'

'Perfectly satisfactory,' declared Santa Spratt. 'Send her over to Mrs Chuffey at the College. I've got an appointment.'

With elastic steps he crossed the courtyard to the surgical block, and took the lift to the Professor's room on the roof.

'Come in!' The Professor looked up testily from his desk, where he was dictating letters into a machine. 'Oh, it's you.'

'Hindehead, will you spare me a minute?'

'I do happen to be rather busy, you know. Arranging a year's absence from the hospital involves an enormous amount of paperwork.'

'I will be brief.' Sir Lancelot made himself comfortable in an armchair. 'And I think I would advise you to turn that tape recorder off. You are not starting your sabbatical year until after the consultants' meeting appointing the new Warden?'

The Professor gave a nod.

'Then I can afford you a few extra days' holiday. The meeting will not now be necessary.'

He looked up. 'What, you mean you're withdrawing your application?'

Sir Lancelot placed his fingertips together. 'Precisely.'

A smile spread across the Professor's smooth features. 'My dear Lancelot, this is a Christmas present indeed. Of course, I realized that with your natural sagacity and reasonableness you'd reach that conclusion sooner or later. I only ask you,' he added kindly, 'not to think of it in any way as a personal victory for myself.'

'I mean no meeting will be necessary as I have already been appointed.' He threw a letter on the desk. 'It's from old Lady Turtle.'

The Professor's smile went off at the mains.

'But Lady Turtle has refused to see a soul since her husband died years ago. That's why the hospital administers the entire Turtle Bequest.'

'She didn't refuse to see me,' returned Sir Lancelot sticking out his legs. 'You may not be aware that the deeds founding the College specifically leave the appointment of Warden in the hands of the Turtle family. After all the take-over bids, she's the only one left.'

'Lancelot!' The Professor leapt up. 'This is a dastardly and unworthy trick. You merely went behind your colleagues' back and got this old lady to appoint you.'

'She didn't appoint me. Charlie did.'

Professor Hindehead frowned. 'Charlie?'

'Yes. I was mystified during my visit to Lady Turtle's country house by her constant references to Charlie. He seemed to be an Indian gentleman. An odd name for a Hindu, possibly. I suspected some *affaire de coeur* – after all, even rather elderly ladies can still have fun. Particularly if they are extremely rich. All decisions were referred to Charlie. After dinner I was invited to meet him.'

'Lancelot, I don't know if this is some sort of elaborate joke – '

'A table was prepared. The butler was summoned – funny little man, like a monkey in a tail coat. The lights were lowered. I held hands with the pair of them across the table. Lady Turtle went into a trance and started bellowing for Charlie. It was very weird, I assure you.'

'You must be out of your mind to imagine this trickery – '

'Charlie eventually came on the line, and I was approved. There's the letter to confirm it,' he added, rising. 'The gift of the Wardenship is entirely in my hands. Personally, I think the old trout was gratified that anyone from the hospital which spends so much of her money should take the trouble to come down and see her. Good morning. And – ' Sir Lancelot remembered at the door, 'Merry Christmas.'

He strode delightedly along the top floor corridor. On the day of the Varsity match he had really been indifferent about the Wardenship, which would complicate his life with idiots like Randolph Nightrider and play the devil with his fishing in summer. But once he foresaw it snatched away by Professor Hindehead, he applied to his election the same determination that performed abdominal operations of a scope still whispered about awesomely in the wards of St Swithin's.

Sir Lancelot spent the whole day spreading sweetness round the hospital from the Air Pollution Unit on the roof to the X-ray department in the basement. His ebullience simmered down only as he crossed the road again after tea in the refectory and found a Rover outside the College emitting Mr & Mrs George Nightrider.

'Good grief,' he muttered. 'I'd completely forgotten those leeches were anchoring themselves for Christmas.'

'Merry Christmas,' called Mr Nightrider, with a quickly manufactured smile. 'How gratifying it is, Lancelot, to find our families coming together at this time of the year.'

'H'm,' said Sir Lancelot.

'Ah, Randolph, there you are,' he added, spotting his son trying to slip past from the College doorway.

'Hello, Dad.' Randolph stood on one leg. 'Hello, Ma.' He stood on the other one. It was his first meeting with his parents since the reception. 'Merry Christmas.'

'What on earth have you got in your hand?' demanded Mr Nightrider severely.

'This? Oh, it's a blunt instrument. For the play we're doing. I'm the prop manager. I was just nipping across for the dress rehearsal.'

'You will not nip anywhere before you have carried our cases in. I am glad I was spared referring to your disgraceful behaviour the other night,' he continued, as Randolph obliged, 'after Sir Lancelot's assurance on the telephone that he had administered the lecture of a lifetime and gated you for a year.'

'Oh, has he?' asked Randolph, looking puzzled.

Sir Lancelot changed the subject. 'Your son is now the proud possessor of a new car.'

'Yes, lovely little MG with discs and modified carbs.,' he announced, brightening up.

'I only hope you saved the money honestly,' Mr Nightrider told him bleakly. 'I should not like to think you were indulging in selling second-hand cars on commission, or anything like that.'

'Of course not,' concurred Sir Lancelot.

'You must behave yourself now, you know, Randolph, as I am so shortly to be given the Min – minimum of latitude,' he added mysteriously. 'I am delighted my sister kindly afforded us this invitation,' he continued, accompanying Sir Lancelot towards the study while his wife followed their son upstairs with the cases. 'The hospital background, you know, particularly at Christmas. It will so create the right "image", as they say, when I take over the Ministry of Health in a week or so. I have asked a young man to come along on Christmas Day and take photographs for the newspapers. Doubtless there are a few bedridden old ladies in the hospital who would quite enjoy my calling to shake hands with them.'

'You can kiss 'em under the mistletoe as far as I'm concerned.'

'By the way, I learnt the Ministry had an enquiry about that rude young fellow Moneypenny. Do you know Colonel Lexington? He was at that reception.'

'Colonel RAMC? Yes, very well. Asks me to guest nights at Millbank.'

'He wanted to get in touch with the man again rather urgently, and I said I would arrange a meeting just as soon as I took over.'

'Old Etonian dinner or something, I suppose,' murmured Sir Lancelot, opening the door and revealing Marylin Shufflewell sucking a lollipop in the middle of the carpet.

'My dear young lady, you can't suck lollipops in here,' the surgeon declared. 'Our guest under the Christmas Child scheme,' he introduced her to his brother-in-law.

'Excellent, excellent!' Mr Nightrider gave the child a saintly smile. 'It will certainly not detract from the "image". Are you enjoying your sweet, my dear?'

'Yes, thank you.'

'Here is a penny,' he added, with the air of a saint issuing haloes to the new intake.

'Who the devil's that?' demanded Sir Lancelot, noticing a youth in narrow trousers, pointed boots, and an elaborate hair-do asleep in the big armchair by the fire.

'My bruvver Arnold,' Marylin enlightened him.

'Well your bruvver Arnold can damn well find another doss-house. Hey, you!' he roared. 'What the hell do you think you're doing here?'

Arnold rubbed his eyes. ' 'Ullo. I came to see my sister,' he explained, yawning.

'Well, now you've seen her you can go home again. She isn't travelling on a party ticket.'

'That's the trouble, Guv'nor,' he announced, standing up and adjusting the piece of black string round his neck. 'You see, I ain't got nowhere to go.'

Sir Lancelot glared. 'A child of your age could fend for himself, I should imagine.'

'It's like this, Guv'nor,' Arnold explained. 'I'm a member of the League of Young Christian Soldiers. Look, here's me badge. We goes round doing good, you see. Old folk, sick, crippled, 'andicapped – all that lot. Takes all my spare time, it does.'

'That must be *most* rewarding,' beamed Mr Nightrider.

'Oh, no,' Arnold contradicted him. 'We don't take a penny for it. All volunt'ry. I was staying with our Vicar over Christmas. To be right handy for the job, like.' He looked solemnly at his pointed toes. 'But the poor gen'leman passed away. This very morning.'

'Dear me!' exclaimed Mr Nightrider. 'It must have been a terrible shock.'

'No, it was nat'rul causes,' Arnold assured him. 'Old age, and that. 'Course, it put the stopper on our Christmas programme. We was going to cheer up the local incurables.'

'But my dear young man, you must stay here,' declared Mr Nightrider. 'Surely you can fit him in somewhere, Lancelot? These days it is a pleasure to award such virtue in our youth.'

'Oh, all right, all right,' declared the host impatiently. 'The little girl can take him down to Mrs Chuffey. I now ask for a little time alone. I have a great deal of important work to finish before the holiday.'

Once by himself, Sir Lancelot settled in the big armchair and reached for GEM Skues' *Minor Tactics of the Chalk Stream*. The grey skies cleared away outside as he drifted gently into that bewitching land of softly gurgling water, buttercup-spotted meadows, trees cooling their fingers in the lazy current, contentedly ruminating cows, swooping birds and plopping trout, which materializes for the magic rod of the fisherman. Perhaps he drifted even further into a light doze, because he suddenly looked up to find another young man and a girl of about eighteen eyeing him from the doorway.

'Get out,' Sir Lancelot greeted them.

'Sorry, mate,' apologized the young man. 'But we was looking for the Warder.'

'I am, thank Providence, not your mate. And I can't imagine why you could possibly want to see me.'

'The thin gentleman sent us in,' explained the girl. 'Him with the forehead. I've come to see my little sister.'

'Good grief, not another,' he muttered. 'I expect you'll find her in the kitchen eating something.'

'Yeah...' The young man looked hesitant. 'But it's like this, you see, mister. Me and me wife ain't got nowhere to go.'

'I am not running the ruddy Dorchester Hotel,' roared Sir Lancelot, rising. 'I am extremely sorry if you are homeless, but we are fully booked. Good afternoon.'

'We was evicted, mister.' The young man looked pitiful. 'On Christmas Eve.'

'I have had the pleasure of your acquaintance for only ten seconds, but I feel assured it was fully justified.'

' 'Artless, it was. Dead 'artless.'

'Just because I'm going to have a baby,' added the wife, starting to sob.

Sir Lancelot shot her a keen glance. 'You don't look as though you're going to have a baby to *me*.'

'Be a bit o' time yet, o' course,' the man explained. 'But our landlord was very particular.'

'The gentleman with the forehead said we could stay,' appealed the wife tearfully. 'And we've brought in the luggage.'

'All right, all right!' snapped Sir Lancelot. 'Move in for life if you like, but don't you damn well get in *my* hair. Who's that?' he demanded shortly as a middle-aged lady in a red hat appeared behind them.

'Why, it's Ma!' exclaimed the wife, brightening up. 'Hello, Ma.'

'Hello, Milly. Hello, Greg. Why, there's little Marylin and Arnold,' she exclaimed, as the other two appeared with Mr Nightrider. 'Isn't that nice now? All together, just at Christmas.'

'My dear Lancelot,' beamed the future Minister of Health. 'Surely you will seize this wonderful chance of bringing happiness to so many lives? Mrs Shufflewell here found herself quite inconsolable without her little girl over Christmas. Do you realize she made the sacrifice of sending dear Marylin from their own little home, so the child could enjoy the delights of your more opulent household? Obviously, you must let the mother stay too. As for the dastardly treatment meted out to this young couple by their landlord, I can only say that I will certainly take the strongest action once I am installed in the Min – the miniver,' he ended obscurely.

'Let them all in,' bellowed Sir Lancelot. 'I'm going to spend Christmas alone at the club.'

'Really, Lancelot, I should expect you to be rather more charitable,' his brother-in-law admonished him. 'Surely it does your eyes good to see this little group radiant with happiness?'

'Not in the slightest. How do you imagine there'll be enough bath water?'

'Wouldn't it be lovely,' suggested Mrs Shufflewell, while little Marylin was being passed round and kissed, 'if only we could have Pop with us?'

'Oh, wouldn't it!' cried everyone at once.

'He has to be away so much,' she explained in Mr Nightrider's direction.

'My dear lady, someone must bear the burden of our commercial enterprises, or our country would perish.'

'Now, isn't that nice?' asked Mrs Shufflewell in general. 'Yes, bear the burden, that's what poor Pop does. Still, we'll think of him.'

Everyone agreed they'd think of him.

'I'm sure we shall have an excellent Christmas,' continued Mr Nightrider. 'Perhaps tomorrow you will all have your photographs taken with me? Good! They might even be in the newspapers, you know, the day I move into the Min – minstrels' gallery. Where are you going, Lancelot?'

'The Thames,' said the surgeon, and slammed the door.

11

Sir Lancelot did not go into the Thames. He went into the King George public house next door.

'A large malt whisky, if you please, Pat,' he grunted. 'I shall probably be spending the entire Christmas in here.'

'Something the matter, Sir Lancelot?' she asked solicitously. 'You should be allowed to enjoy Christmas in your own home.'

'I could enjoy Christmas in any other Salvation Army hostel, but not if I were footing the bill as well.'

He picked up an evening paper from the bar.

'H'm, those blasted Associated Metal shares have been bounding ahead since the take-over. Pity I sold out. Aren't you and that young man of yours off for a gay time somewhere?' he asked suddenly. 'Getting married next week, I should have thought you'd be up to the ears in muslin and orange blossom, and that sort of thing.'

'I've got to help out over Christmas,' explained Pat, polishing a glass. 'I can't let the boss down, can I?'

Sir Lancelot sipped his whisky.

'Besides,' she added, arranging a dish of crisps, 'I think Clive wants to work over the holiday. He says everything's coming to a climax in the lab.'

Sir Lancelot felt for his pipe.

'And anyway,' Pat ended, wiping a splash from the counter, 'it's all off.'

'Off?' demanded Sir Lancelot.

'It was a crazy idea, really, I suppose.' She went on wiping. 'One of

Clive's real mad ones. It could never have worked out.'

'Rubbish,' said Sir Lancelot.

'His friends couldn't take me,' Pat continued, wiping away. 'Not that I cared. Oh, not a bit. It was water off a duck's back. Honest, it was, Sir Lancelot. But I'd only have held up Clive's career at the hospital. So I told him this morning we'd best go our own ways.'

'But damn it, girl!' complained the surgeon. 'He'll be in an absolutely pitiful state without you. How about his laundry?'

'It's all for the best,' declared Pat, transferring the wiping operations to her eye.

'Have a drink,' offered Sir Lancelot shortly.

They were interrupted by the entire male cast of the College play, arriving to fortify themselves for the performance. This was in defiance of their producer's orders, McWhittle having called everyone on stage after the dress rehearsal and announced, 'Don't forget, ladies and gentlemen, that you have lines to remember tonight. I've no wish to sound a spoil-sport, but I don't want any of you sneaking out to the pub before we bring up the curtain. We're putting this show on for the enjoyment of the audience, not of ourselves. If you're feeling a bit nervous, remember that pros never touch a drop before going on. It's in their contracts,' he added knowingly.

'Ah, the hempen home-spuns,' quoted Sir Lancelot, transferring his attention to the students. 'Gentlemen, I am in the chair.'

His offer was received with more than usual enthusiasm, most of the players being in fact highly nervous indeed, particularly Filthy Fred. Shortly after Fred assumed Randolph's part, his colleague LaSage, who had an eye for these things, dismissed Susan as an uphill struggle. Tossing aside his advantages as her lover for three hours solidly, with intervals, LaSage concentrated instead on the pretty snub-nosed speech therapist who had been co-opted to play the maid. With McWhittle burning slowly with passion like a Scottish joss-stick safely beyond the footlights, Filthy Fred was left a free run with the leading lady on stage. By Christmas Eve he was desperately in love with her. As her murdered husband, he was determined to give the performance of his life until his death. Taking prophylaxis against his appearance being ruined by stage fright he had already downed several vodkas, a drink to which he was not usually given, but he didn't want to smell when he kissed her.

'You will have a good house in the stalls, anyway,' Sir Lancelot assured the players as Pat silently distributed the drinks. 'Apart from the Nightriders, I shall be bringing a peculiar family who seem to have confused me with Father Christmas. Where is young Randolph, by the way?' he enquired, looking round. 'It's unlike him to miss a free drink.'

'Checking his props, sir,' explained Filthy Fred, reaching for another vodka. 'He says he doesn't care for supper in College this evening.'

'That makes two of us,' nodded Sir Lancelot.

Randolph was in fact sitting alone on a property sofa on the dim-lit stage adding up his overtime on the wages of sin.

'Five hundred quid commish from Sir L,' he was calculating with a pencil on the back of his property plot. 'Less a hundred to old Clingy for the intro, and two hundred in the Post Office for a rainy day…' He scratched his head. 'Two hundred nicker on Hullabaloo at Uttoxeter at twenty to one, plus stake money, four thousand two hundred…less six hundred for the MG… three thousand quid in Associated Metals standing at thirty-five bob, capital gain to date fifteen hundred smackers… By golly!'

His mind reeled at the prospect of such riches. But he stuffed the paper back in his pocket with a sigh. Like many men before, he asked himself the use of wealth when the only object he wanted was beyond money to buy. It was galling the way Filthy Fred had taken up with Susan Grantchester.

Randolph got up and wandered below the stage to the cubby-hole where he kept his properties. He found McWhittle inside sitting on a wicker hamper with a bottle of whisky.

'Hello,' exclaimed Randolph. 'What's up? Sort of second-hand stage fright?'

'That swine Filthy Fred,' the producer growled. 'I've half a mind to bash his ruddy face in just as soon as we don't need it any more for the show.'

'Go on?' Randolph asked, trying to look innocent. 'What's the trouble? Isn't he giving an adequate performance?'

McWhittle produced a laugh like something jamming in a piece of heavy machinery. 'His performance is too damn adequate, that's what. Have a drink,' he offered thickly.

Like many blustery young men, alcohol produced an effect on him with enviable economy.

'Disgusting, that's the only word,' McWhittle continued, as Randolph poured Johnnie Walker into one of the property glasses. 'With Susan. Pretty well raping her in full view of the audience.'

'Perhaps you're just imagining it, old cock?' Randolph tried to console him.

'Imagining? That blasted man doesn't leave *anything* to the imagination.' The producer stuck out a hand. 'Shake, old man. After all, you were once after her, too.'

'How on earth did you suspect?' demanded Randolph.

McWhittle took another gulp. 'Did you get anywhere?' he enquired.

'Eh…not actually,' confessed Randolph, after a silence. 'Did you?' he added after another one.

'At first she seemed quite attracted to me,' explained McWhittle, as though describing an interesting case in the wards. 'But last night she… she told me to take my dirty great hands off her,' he ended miserably into his glass.

'Can't imagine what Susan sees in a neolithic specimen like Fred,' speculated Randolph. 'Perhaps it's the way his ears stick out.'

'The way they nuzzle on that sofa before my very eyes!' McWhittle continued bitterly. 'It's a wonder the audience don't lose the thread of the plot. I'd like to take the blunt instrument to *him* and no mistake.'

'Look, old cock,' Randolph pointed out handsomely. 'Why don't you have a go at the speech therapist and make Susan jealous?'

He shook his head sadly. 'There is only one Susan. And anyway, the other girl's voice gives me the willies.'

Sir Lancelot dined that night off a tray in his study, explaining he was overwhelmed with work. Just before eight he gathered Mr and Mrs Nightrider, Lady Spratt, and the Shufflewell family in the Lodge hall.

'I'm sure we're going to amuse ourselves immensely,' smiled Mr Nightrider to Ma, taking charge of proceedings as usual. 'Are you fond of the theatre, Mrs Shufflewell?'

'Many's a *lovely* cry I've had when Pop used to take me in the old days. He does enjoy a theatre so, does Pop. What a pity he can't be here tonight.'

The others agreed it was a real shame.

'Enjoying your lollipop, little girl?' beamed Mr Nightrider.

'Yes, thank you.'

'I'm really quite glad to see Randolph taking an interest in amateur theatricals, Lancelot,' he added, as his brother-in-law opened the street door. 'I was always most keen on them myself. But of course such activities are out of the question now I am to become a Min – mincepie consumer.'

'Why,' cried Ma, as a fat, sporty-looking man in a check waistcoat came hurrying up the steps. 'There's Pop.'

'Hello, Pop!' cried the Shufflewells.

'So you got away,' exclaimed Ma, as he gave kisses all round. 'How nice!'

'I'm absolutely delighted you could be reunited with your family over Christmas,' announced Mr Nightrider, warmly introducing himself. 'This is Sir Lancelot Spratt, a distinguished medical gentleman.'

'Great honour to meet you, sir,' asserted Mr Shufflewell. 'I have the greatest respect for the medical profession, sir. It has given me a very great deal in the past, sir.'

'I think we should get out of the cold,' was all Sir Lancelot could manage to mutter. 'Unless, Mr Shufflewell, you happen to have another busload of relatives round the corner?'

'This is the lot, sir. Just one happy family.'

'A happy family indeed!' smiled Mr Nightrider.

'How nice!' concurred Ma.

'What is this exacting business of yours, Mr Shufflewell?' added Mr Nightrider as they crossed the street.

'I am a dealer, sir.'

'Oh, really? What sort of dealer?'

'You might say a general dealer, sir.'

'How interesting,' murmured Mr Nightrider. 'And now the play's the thing,' he declared, as they entered the crowded Founders' Hall.

About two-thirds of the audience were staff and patients and the rest local inhabitants, who were staring at the fantastic contraptions round sufferers from the orthopaedic wards and feeling anything on the stage would be an anti-climax. The students in the auditorium were already singing *Why Are we Waiting?*, and broke into ironical cheers, smilingly acknowledged by Mr Nightrider, as Sir Lancelot led in his party. The surgeon took a seat in the middle of the front row next to his brother-in-law and lit a cigar, in a thoroughly bad temper.

The slow handclap broke out as the Secretary of the St Swithin's Musical Society, who backstage had already played records of the overtures from *Orpheus in the Underworld* and *William Tell* three times each, gave them a fourth offering. There was a flash from the footlights in front of Sir Lancelot's nose as a bulb blew out. Shiverings of the curtain announced somebody peering anxiously at the opposition. A roar acclaimed the dimming of the houselights, but immediately they went up again. Nobody in the audience was particularly disturbed by all this. It was exactly the same every year.

'There would seem to be some hitch backstage,' murmured Mr Nightrider, looking at his watch.

Nobody could find Filthy Fred.

'Have you looked in his room?' demanded McWhittle wildly to Randolph. 'And in all the lavs? I suppose he couldn't possibly be in the King George or somewhere drinking?'

'Absolutely sunk without trace, old cock.'

'Not a word to Susan,' he enjoined urgently. 'She's a very sensitive performer.'

After ten minutes they had a phone call to say Fred was being sick in Casualty.

'It's all right,' Filthy Fred muttered, while Randolph and McWhittle rubbed carmine make-up on his ashen cheeks. 'It was vodka, so no one can tell from my breath.'

Sir Lancelot was halfway through his cigar, with his mind on Clive Moneypenny and Pat. He hoped the idiotic girl hadn't jilted him just because of Deirdre Ivors-Smith's poisonous lunch party. You may be wondering – quite as much as the couple themselves – why Sir Lancelot should take such a fatherly interest in them. But he too was once in love with the barmaid in the King George. Her name was Rose, she wore flame-coloured dresses and silk stockings with clocks on them, and they used to Charleston together wildly. One night he took her to see Tallulah Bankhead and nearly proposed to her afterwards in the taxi. But unlike Clive he hadn't the courage. She married the gin traveller, and though Sir Lancelot felt things probably more in order by his later marrying little Miss Nightrider, he now reflected that Rose might at least have brought him a reasonable brother-in-law.

'Now the fun begins,' declared Mr Nightrider, as the hall was abruptly plunged into pitch darkness and the curtain went up.

The footlights flashed on to illuminate the first scene between the chauffeur and the maid. As the chauffeur was a squat, black-browed totally inaudible student known as The Hunk, and as the speech therapist playing the maid threw bell-like words to the furthest limits of the hall, they struck the audience as an odd pair of domestics. As they disappeared and Susan tripped on in riding habit, Randolph stationed himself worshipfully in the wings. He felt a jog, and saw McWhittle beside him offering a drink.

'Taste that!' hissed the producer.

'By golly!' exclaimed Randolph. 'Cold tea.' Their eyes strayed to the bottle of Johnnie Walker on the sideboard, awaiting Filthy Fred's entrance. 'I must have mixed the two bottles up,' Randolph confessed. 'That one on stage is yours.'

'Is that you, darling?' called Susan.

'Who else?' demanded Filthy Fred, coming through the French windows and kissing her with a more preoccupied air than usual. 'I need a drink,' he announced, pouring half a tumbler from the bottle and swallowing it.

The audience roared at the magnificent splutter.

'Very comic,' smiled Mr Nightrider to Sir Lancelot. 'I doubt if Jimmy Edwards could do better.'

'Where have you been, my love?' Filthy Fred went on, managing to focus on Susan.

'Where do I ever go?' she replied coolly.

'I wouldn't be surprised if you'd met young Derrington again in the woods,' he declared suspiciously.

'Oh?' she asked indifferently.

'I'm going to have another drink,' he told her brutally.

'I never thought I'd end up married to an alcoholic,' she declaimed bitterly.

Filthy Fred took the second whisky more slowly.

'Where have you been, my love?' he enquired.

'Where do I ever go?' she replied coolly.

'I wouldn't be surprised if you'd met young Derrington in the woods,' he declared suspiciously.

'Oh?' she asked indifferently.

'I'm going to have another drink,' he told her brutally.

'I never thought I'd end up married to an alcoholic,' she declaimed bitterly.

'Where have you been, my love?' he asked after the third one.

At the end of a long silence Susan hissed, 'We've done that bit.'

'I beg your pardon?' asked Filthy Fred politely.

'We've just *done it*.'

'Oh. Sorry. I'm going to have another drink,' he announced after a pause, and fell on his face.

The curtain came down to uproarious applause.

'Dear me,' exclaimed Mr Nightrider. 'The poor fellow's fainted.'

Then they had *Orpheus in the Underworld* and *William Tell* over again.

'Ladies and gentlemen,' announced McWhittle, appearing before the curtain a few minutes later looking quite as pale as Filthy Fred. 'I'm afraid Mr Forcedyke is indisposed – '

Roars of, 'Is there a doctor in the house?'

'And his part will be taken over at short notice by Mr Randolph Nightrider. We'll start again from the beginning.'

'My son,' whispered Mr Nightrider proudly to Pop Shufflewell on his other side. 'I always say he's best in an emergency.'

'I'm enjoying this, and no mistake,' declared Pop warmly.

'Next year I'm going to spend Christmas in bed,' muttered Sir Lancelot.

Randolph made his entrance standing on one leg and advanced on Susan. As soon as he kissed her, he knew he was in business.

12

'Merry Christmas, my dear,' Sir Lancelot addressed Lady Spratt at seven the next morning, producing from a secret hiding-place in his bedside cupboard a pair of gold and ruby earrings.

'Merry Christmas, my love,' returned Lady Spratt, producing from a secret hiding-place in her wardrobe a large box from Harrod's.

Sir Lancelot opened it to find a couple of bright silk T-shirts, tropical trousers, swimming trunks, sandals, and a sporty light straw hat.

'Come in useful during the summer, I'm sure,' he thanked her gruffly. He had been hoping for a box of cigars. 'I think I'll have my bacon and eggs up here this morning,' he added, starting the business of the day.

'Oh, dear me, no, Lancelot. Cornflakes only, I'm afraid. With all those peculiar Shufflewell people lodging in the students' rooms the cook's liable to walk out any minute.'

'On Christmas Day?' he scowled. 'It's unthinkable.'

'She's an unthinkable cook. I told you she was a paranoic. She had delusions that Randolph harboured designs on her kitchen maid.'

'That young man needs some sort of operation,' muttered Sir Lancelot. 'I presume we shall have a Christmas dinner?'

'Eight o'clock in Hall, if I have to cook it myself,' Lady Spratt promised.

When Sir Lancelot finally came downstairs to be greeted by Pop Shufflewell and Mr Nightrider, he began to feel that Scrooge may have had a point after all.

'Merry Christmas, my dear Lancelot,' Mr Nightrider called round the decorated tree. 'You really must witness the splendid act of seasonable charity being performed by our excellent Mr Shufflewell here.'

'And a very merry Christmas to you, sir,' added Pop Shufflewell, sticking his thumbs in his waistcoat. 'As you know, sir, I am a general dealer, and I was very lucky being able to get my hands on a few seasonable commodities.'

He indicated several dozen cases of wine stacked in the hall, inspected solemnly by little Marylin sucking two lollipops at once.

'These goodies, Sir Lancelot, would be my pleasure to give the poor people suffering in the hospital opposite.' The expectant couple, Greg and Milly, staggered through the door with another case. 'Put it down careful, Greg boy, it's valuable.'

'Naturally, I do not approve the widespread consumption of alcoholic drink,' indicated Mr Nightrider, 'but at Christmas I'm sure the patients will greatly appreciate a glass of claret with their dinner. Unfortunately, the National Health Service does not allow more than a bottle of brown ale to celebrate the festival. I shall certainly look into the regulations once I am in charge of the Min – minions,' he ended vacantly.

'You're being generous with a damn good year,' grunted Sir Lancelot. 'That's Lynch Bages fifty-five, isn't it?'

'I can see you're a connoisseur, sir. I have reserved these cases here for your festive table tonight.'

'I think it would be best if I made the distribution myself,' decided Mr Nightrider, accompanying Sir Lancelot into the Warden's study. 'Mr Shufflewell would be quite lost in St Swithin's. My photographer will no doubt wish to record the happy occasion. By the way,' he added, as the surgeon shut the door, 'I suppose that bumptious young man Moneypenny will be in the hospital today for the general jollifications?'

'I think it extremely unlikely he'll be within miles of the place.'

'Oh. Pity.' Mr Nightrider looked disappointed. 'You see, I'd rather like to appear with him as one of my protégés when I take over the Ministry. It all helps, you know.'

Sir Lancelot frowned. 'If you wish to stretch the seasonal goodwill like corset elastic, I suppose it's your affair.'

'Of course, his work is terribly important. At least, that's what Colonel

Lexington says. I wouldn't know. I am an administrator, not a technician.'

Sir Lancelot tugged his beard. 'Important? Struck me about as relevant to clinical medicine as the measurements of the Great Pyramid.'

'My dear Lancelot, you can be frank with *me*.' He helped himself to one of his brother-in-law's cigars. 'Please remember I shall soon stand at the pinnacle of the Health Service. It's about this nerve gas.'

'What nerve gas?' demanded Sir Lancelot shortly.

'You mean you don't know?' Mr Nightrider looked pained. 'All happening in your own hospital, too. I hope you will not think me overstepping the bounds of family courtesy by expressing a little surprise.' He struck one of Sir Lancelot's matches. 'You know the Army have this gas which paralyses people? Curare-like, I believe you call it. Your anaesthetists use the drug by injection, I understand.' He blew a puff of smoke. 'Well, young Moneypenny has found the antidote.'

'Good grief!' muttered Sir Lancelot. 'After the holiday I'd certainly better get hold of – what the devil are you doing there?' he broke off to young Arnold, asleep in the big chair by the fire.

'Oh! Sorry, Guv'nor.' He stretched. 'Didn't kip very well last night. Insomnia. I'm a martyr to it.'

'As far as I'm concerned you can sink into a profound coma until Boxing night, as long as you don't do it in *my* presence. Now get out.'

'Sure, Guv'nor.' He shuffled his feet. 'Wouldn't like to make a Christmas donation for our poor friendless old folk, would you?'

'I happen to be one of them. Now if you will kindly all leave me in peace, I can get through some pressing work before appearing at midday to be jolly in the wards.'

It was traditional at St Swithin's on Christmas morning for the consultants to breeze cheerfully among any patients unlucky enough to be locked up in the place, in the spirit that Army officers serve their men's turkey and pud. As Simon Sparrow drove Nikki and his four-year-old son through the crisp sunshine, he felt he wasn't in a mood to breeze cheerfully among even a gala night of the Bacchanalian revels. He'd never remembered a more miserable Christmas. The Ann Beverley affair lingered, even after Nikki accepted he wasn't on the point of eloping with her to Reno. His wife was, in fact, being very brave about it, often observing as she dished out his supper, 'Of course, I am only a housewife. You can't expect me to go round like some glamorous film star when I've a house to run and a child to look after *and* a couple of clinics a week in the local reform school.' He found this particularly irritating, which was reasonable, as she intended it to be.

Much more depressing was Dr Defoe and his five thousand pounds.

'As a second mortgage on the house raises more laughs than Norman Wisdom,' he announced, driving his Mini into the St Swithin's courtyard, 'I shall have to fire the final shot in the locker.'

'Which is?'

'I shall try and borrow the money from Ann Beverley.'

'You will *not* try and borrow the money from Ann Beverley!'

Simon shrugged his shoulders.

'Now the locker looks like Mother Hubbard's cupboard, I'll come up with a suggestion,' declared Nikki.

'Which is?'

'You'll try and borrow the money from Sir Lancelot Spratt.'

'I will certainly *not* try and borrow the money from Sir Lancelot Spratt!' He looked for somewhere to park.

'Well, at least you might ask him for advice,' Nikki backed down.

'Rather difficult when we haven't been on speaking terms for a week.'

'Perhaps today he'll be radiating the Christmas spirit?'

'Anything Sir Lancelot radiates in my direction I wouldn't touch with the end of a Geiger counter,' ended Simon, switching off the engine.

Simon found the senior surgeon jovial enough, watching Mr Nightrider being photographed handing a bottle of claret to a mystified old lady, who believed it was all some new form of treatment.

'Ah, Simon, there you are,' Sir Lancelot boomed. 'Merry Christmas. By the way, my boy,' he added, digging him in the ribs, 'I'll save you the bother and indignity of trying to fix the committee over the Wardenship. I happen to have clinched it already.'

'Oh, really?' Simon had totally forgotten about such trivial business in the past few days.

'I'm afraid, young man, you will have to know a trick or two more before taking on a seasoned campaigner like me,' Sir Lancelot beamed at him.

Simon licked his lips. His situation was too desperate for the luxury of pride. The old boy certainly seemed in a cracking mood. And even if he simply bit his head from his shoulders, it would be one down for his wife.

'Sir Lancelot – I wonder if I could have a word with you? In private?'

'As many as you like. But I told you the Wardenship business is wholly settled.'

'No, it's something else. I think I shall have to resign from the St Swithin's staff.'

'Indeed?' Sir Lancelot tugged his beard. 'Professional misconduct with that actress woman, I suppose?'

'Oh, heavens, no! Well, yes, I suppose so.' Simon looked awkward. 'Could we step across to your Lodge?'

Across the broad desk in the Warden's study, Simon again poured out the story of Dr Defoe.

'H'm,' concluded Sir Lancelot. 'Yes, I know this Defoe feller well enough. Been trying to get him run in for months. Can't touch him, of course. A dangerous trickster. Someone ought to warn the public against him.'

'I did, and look where it's got me,' complained Simon.

'He's agreed to come down to five thousand?'

Simon nodded. 'I was wondering…I mean, I really am in a hole…oh, it's an outrageous suggestion, I suppose, and I only hope you'll forgive me…but do you think you could make me a loan of it?'

'Naturally,' nodded Sir Lancelot. 'Would you care for a glass of Maderia?'

Simon stared at him. 'But I thought you thoroughly disliked me?' he burst out.

'My dear boy, I disliked you far more as a snotty-nosed student. Do you recall when you were before me on a Disciplinary Committee, after an affray involving a pinched ambulance, several members of the nursing staff, a stuffed animal of indeterminate species called, if I recall, Hubert, and apparently the entire Metropolitan Police Force? Mainly on Hindehead's insistence you were fined twenty-five pounds – a fortune to an impoverished medical student. Who paid it?'

Simon smiled. 'You did.'

'One should always stick to one's principles, don't you think?'

Sir Lancelot rose and made for the drinks cupboard. 'I will let you have my cheque in the – what the devil are you doing here?' he snapped, finding Pop Shufflewell dozing in the big armchair.

'Dear me, I must have dropped off. Begging your pardon, I'm sure, sir. I always sleep very badly in a strange bed – '

'Get out,' he hissed.

'Very sorry, sir, but I'm not used to the excitement – '

'Get *out!* And if I find any more of your blasted family in here, I'll kick them out before you've had your Christmas dinner. Blasted impertinence,' he growled as the door shut. 'Luckily, he's such an ignoramus he won't have understood a thing. I'll need the loan repaid some time, Simon.'

'But of course, sir.'

'Meanwhile, you might give me your opinion on a glass of this Solera sixty-four. I'm rather proud of it. Then you'd better get back before your missus gets hopping mad.'

'Yes, indeed – '

'Oh, and when you do repay you might make your cheque out for five thousand and twenty-five. You never let me have the first one back.'

'Mr Sparrow – ' called Sister Virtue as Simon reached the wards with a feeling of immeasurable relief. The family wouldn't have a holiday for the next ten years and he'd have to run the Mini till the wheels dropped off, but at least he'd avoided leaving St Swithin's under the biggest cloud since the Ark. 'Mr Sparrow, your wife asked me to look after the little boy, as she had to go off.'

'Go off?' Simon frowned.

'Yes, there was a phone call. She said something about seeing a case.'

He shrugged his shoulders. 'Must be riots in the reform school, I suppose.'

'She said she wouldn't be long.'

'Oh, very well. I'll hang about here.'

'Would you like to come into my office for a drink, Mr Sparrow?'

'Very much,' agreed Simon.

He wondered what the devil Nikki was up to now.

13

'Lancelot,' announced Lady Spratt, as he was blotting the cheque soon after Simon's departure. 'There's a pretty girl outside asking for you. Do you want to see her?'

'My dear Maud, after thirty years of married life, what a question.'

She showed Pat into the study.

'He's gone,' Pat said at once.

Sir Lancelot raised his eyebrows. 'Who's gone?'

'Clive. He's disappeared.'

'What on earth do you mean? He's probably decided to spend Christmas with his family.'

'He hasn't got any family.' Pat sat in the big armchair distractedly. 'Only some brothers in Brazil, I think. I took round the laundry to his digs this morning – after all, he can't be without a clean shirt, can he, especially at Christmas – and his landlady said he'd just that minute cleared off.' She stared hard at the fire. 'I think he's gone behind the Iron Curtain,' she declared.

'Ye gods!' Sir Lancelot jumped up. 'Yes, an Old Etonian – they do that sort of thing in droves.'

'He's left a couple of letters.' Pat opened her bag. 'I went up to his room. It was terribly untidy and he seemed to have taken hardly anything with him. I was rummaging round all sorts of junk and things in bottles, when I saw the envelopes on the mantelpiece. I think he meant to post them, but forgot. You know what Clive's like. One was for me… ' She hesitated. 'You don't want to see it, do you?'

'I will spare your blushes.'

'The other was addressed to you.'

Sir Lancelot tore it open.

'Dear Sir Lancelot, (it said)

'I don't know why I'm sending my resignation to you, but I can't for the life of me think of anyone else who might want it. I am going where I expect to be better appreciated, personally and professionally.

Yours,

Clive Moneypenny.'

Sir Lancelot slammed the letter on the desk.

'That fat Czech feller, he's the villain of the piece. I knew you couldn't trust him. Ought to have had Sandilands kick him out. Has Clive ever talked of doing a bunk?' he asked Pat urgently.

She nodded. 'Often. But he sometimes says outrageous things just to tease people. How he used to make me laugh in the public bar, saying strikers should be sent to Dartmoor – '

'Yes, yes, yes!' Sir Lancelot interrupted. 'But did he have any – well, foreign friends? Embassy people, and all that? You know, fur hats, astrakhan collars, vodka parties, chalk marks on the trees in Hyde Park?'

'He had a few weird friends, but of course I never interfered. I can't see why they should want Clive in Russia, or wherever it is,' she added, looking puzzled. 'He's nothing to do with atoms, and that.'

'Pat – I can't explain, but if it's the last thing I do I've got to stop that man before he crosses the frontier.' He crashed one fist into another. 'By God!' he went on, as she looked alarmed. 'I must get Nightrider to call the Foreign Office at once. No, that won't do. As a private citizen, no one in the world can detain the feller. When did he skip? Ten o'clock. Very cunning. Christmas Day, just the moment to shoot the moon, with the entire country half fuddled from morning to night. If only we could get some faint clue which way he's gone,' he ended desperately.

'Oh, he's gone to Dublin,' Pat informed him. 'By the two o'clock plane. He'd forgotten the receipt for his ticket with the letters.'

'Dublin? Once he's there, of course, he might just as well be locked up in the blasted Kremlin.' He pulled out his watch. 'Good grief, it's nearly one. Come on, my girl, we're off to London Airport. Yes, I know you're busy in the pub, but Mrs Chuffey can take over. After twenty years in my personal service she can turn her hand to anything. Damn! I've only that blasted bubble car,' he remembered, hurrying her across the hall. 'Never do it in the time. Hey! You!' he shouted to Randolph Nightrider, who was helping Susan Grantchester into his shining MG. 'Get that woman out of there. I'm commandeering your car. Don't blather, boy. You'll probably get a medal for it in the end. She will anyway be very much better off with you on the top of a crowded bus.'

With Pat beside him, he shot off westwards.

Sir Lancelot was flagged down by the first police car in Knightsbridge.

'Officer, I am a surgeon at St Swithin's Hospital, on my way with a nurse to an urgent case,' he explained promptly.

'No doubt you are, sir, but our job's to try and cut down your work over Christmas. Can I see your licence, please?'

The second car caught him at Hammersmith.

'Officer, I am Sir Lancelot Spratt, the surgeon, and I must hurry to collect a vital drug arriving at London Airport.'

'Sorry, sir, but all the doctors we stop on this stretch seem after the same thing. They must keep quite a stock of it out there. Your licence please.'

The third was on Chiswick flyover.

'Officer,' explained Sir Lancelot, 'I am in a highly embarrassing situation. This young lady with whom I am gallivanting happens to be another man's wife.'

'Well, sir, I suppose we're entitled to a bit of fun at any age. But keep an eye on the clock, the M4's closed from a crash already. Merry Christmas.'

They had just started along the Great West Road when the car broke down.

'That blasted young idiot Nightrider's been tampering with the works!' snorted Sir Lancelot, jumping out. 'We'll have to get a lift.'

'What in?' asked Pat, who was feeling sick.

He glared up and down the road. On Christmas morning it was as quiet as the village high street.

'Here comes a car,' announced Sir Lancelot, stepping into the gutter with thumb cocked.

After half a dozen more had sped past he wiped his face on his yellow silk handkerchief and commanded Pat, 'You try.'

Three more cars disdained them.

'Display your femora,' ordered Sir Lancelot curtly.

'My what!' cried Pat.

'Your legs, woman. No, more than that. That's the ticket,' he added with satisfaction, as a shiny ambulance screeched up.

' 'Fraid I'm not allowed to take riders,' complained the driver, noticing Sir Lancelot as well.

'My dear man, here is five pounds.' The surgeon opened the back doors. 'London Airport, if you please.'

'Suppose I could take you to the Airport turning,' the driver admitted. 'So long as nobody sees. You'd both better lie on the bed under a blanket.'

'Here!' complained Pat. 'I'm certainly not – '

'Don't argue woman,' muttered Sir Lancelot, pushing her inside. 'Just pass me the blanket.'

Evicted at the Airport's road entrance, they climbed almost at once aboard a helpful black van.

'Drop us at the main departure building,' declared Sir Lancelot breathlessly.

'Going there myself.'

'Can't you put your foot down, man?' he muttered, looking nervously at his watch.

'Hardly right trying a ton-up with this,' returned the driver sombrely, nodding towards his load in the back.

Sir Lancelot noticed a card on the dashboard announcing,

CROUCHLEIGH & SONS
FUNERAL DIRECTORS SINCE 1815

'You might put yourself out to oblige me now,' he grumbled. 'After all, in the past I've done a hell of a lot for you.'

Nikki Sparrow had meanwhile driven the Mini from St Swithin's in the same direction.

The telephone call while Simon was touching Sir Lancelot for five thousand pounds had come straight to the ward, being an urgent message about a private patient.

'I think I'd better take it,' Nikki told the nurse. She picked up the instrument. 'Hello?'

'The Marlborough Hotel here. We have been trying to trace Mr Sparrow, the surgeon. Miss Ann Beverley wishes him to call immediately.'

'Oh, does she?' said Nikki. 'Well, you can tell Miss Ann Beverley… ' She paused. 'Mr Sparrow will be round in a couple of shakes,' she ended, banging it down.

If neurotic film stars sent urgently for Harley Street surgeons on Christmas Day, Nikki decided with a brisk tug to her jacket, they can expect to be attended by their locums. She felt the consultation would do the doctor a great deal of good, if not the patient.

But she hesitated before assaulting the Marlborough itself. She felt justified – indeed, impelled – but she wondered if it was quite ethical. First, she considered in the parked Mini, the GP and not the patient should have summoned the consultant. And if even a neurotic film star sends for a surgical specialist, she is not to be fobbed off with a practitioner from the narrower sphere of reform school clinics. The whole expedition was clearly professionally irregular, and she must return to St Swithin's at once and fetch Simon.

She got out of the car and marched towards the hotel.

'I've called to see Miss Ann Beverley,' Nikki announced to the girl at the desk. 'I'm the doctor.'

'Would you like to go straight up, Doctor? The Blenheim suite.'

Nikki made for the lift, imagining the scene upstairs. The fantastically beautiful film star, her famous blonde hair in careful disarray to her shoulders, something slinky in the way of nightwear, and reclining bewitchingly on the pillow with half-shut lids and half-open mouth.

'I'll show her!' Nikki muttered to herself.

She might, of course, Nikki suddenly decided, have a roaring duodenal perforation, then they'd all be in for a difficult Christmas.

The door was opened by a sandy young man with freckles.

'I'm the doctor,' announced Nikki crisply. 'I'm Mrs Sparrow. I'm standing in for my husband, Mr Simon Sparrow. I've come to see Miss Ann Beverley.'

'Doctor, are we sure glad to see *you*,' exclaimed the young man. 'I guess it ain't serious, but it sure is worrying.'

'Perhaps you will take me to the patient?' demanded Nikki primly.

'Sure. Mom!' called the young man through an inner door. 'The doctor's here, Mom. It's a lady.'

'Mom?' Nikki frowned.

In the second bedroom was a worried-looking young woman, and the film star with a baby on her lap.

'Sorry to bust up your Christmas, Doctor,' Ann Beverley greeted her, 'but my little granddaughter here has sure got us bothered. Say, is it right she should be producing these green diapers?'

'Granddaughter!' Nikki's eyebrows shot up. She smiled. 'Miss Beverley, I assure you this is a consultation which will swiftly put everybody's worries at rest. Now let me have a look at the baby.'

The departure building at London Airport was almost empty, with a few lost-looking passengers and a few bored-looking airline staff, and the loudspeaker demanding, as all through the year, that Mr Fluger of Kansas City should go urgently to the reception desk.

'Come on!' snapped Sir Lancelot, hurrying Pat by the hand up the escalator. 'Ireland,' he demanded of the first man in a peaked cap.

'Can't help you, sir. I'm a chauffeur.'

'Ireland!' barked Sir Lancelot to another man.

'Channel six, sir, just leaving.'

'Come on!'

'It *was* Shannon you wanted, sir? Dublin departures from the other building.'

'Come on!' cried Sir Lancelot, grabbing Pat again.

They dived downstairs, ran outside, stumbled among luggage and found themselves facing a doorway labelled DUBLIN DEPARTURES.

'There he is!' exclaimed Pat, seeing Clive disappearing through a door at the far end of the room.

'Thank God!' muttered Sir Lancelot, 'We've got him in time.'

'May I have your boarding cards, please?' smiled a girl in uniform at their elbow.

'Boarding cards? Of course we haven't got any boarding cards.'

'I'm afraid you must have boarding cards,' she pointed out, still smiling, 'or you won't be able to board the plane.'

'But we don't want to board the blasted plane – '

She smiled even more sweetly. It was the largest part of the job, handling misdirected imbeciles. 'You may wave goodbye to passengers from the terrace on the roof, sir.'

'Wave goodbye is exactly what I do *not* want to do to this particular passenger. You must let me through this instant.'

'I'm very sorry, sir.' Her smile broadened. 'But I'm afraid no one's allowed further without a boarding card.'

'Ye gods! Don't you realize, young lady, the man who's just gone through that exit would make Burgess look like the Chairman of the Primrose League?'

'I'm afraid, sir,' she went on smiling, 'we have no passenger on this flight called Burgess. Nor Primrose,' she added, with another smile. 'You may wave goodbye to – '

'Come on!' barked Sir Lancelot, grabbing Pat again. 'Oh, for heaven's sake, woman, stop blubbing. Up these stairs, double quick.'

They leant over the rail of the terrace. Clive was stepping into the bus for the aircraft.

'Clive!' screamed Pat. 'Clive!'

He looked round.

'Clive, I love you.'

'What's that?' he called back.

'I love you, darling.'

'What are you saying?'

'She loves you, darling,' roared Sir Lancelot. 'You blithering idiot.'

Clive shrugged his shoulders. 'I'm just going to Dublin,' he pointed out.

'Don't, Clive, don't!' cried Pat.

'Come here at once,' commanded the surgeon. 'Oh, do stop weeping, woman, it's enough to put the feller off. Moneypenny, you've been appointed Warden of the Medical College,' he declared desperately.

'I've been what?' frowned Clive.

'All aboard, sir,' said the busman.

'You're the new Warden of the Medical College, Moneypenny. Come back this instant.'

'But my luggage is aboard the plane,' Clive objected.

'Great Scott, man! You can have my entire ruddy wardrobe if you feel like it.'

'Now come along, sir,' urged the busman shortly, 'are you coming or going?'

'I've really no idea,' Clive confessed, 'but I shan't be using the ticket.'

'Warden of the Medical College? Me?' frowned Clive, holding Pat's hand in the hired Daimler taking the three back to London. 'But I can't understand it. Or is it some sort of Christmas box for underpaid employees?'

'In a way, I suppose,' grunted Sir Lancelot, who had been sitting wiping his face with the yellow silk handkerchief since leaving the Airport. 'Frankly, Moneypenny, the powers that be – I needn't specify – felt that your work on muscle physiology attracted far less than the appreciation it deserved. The Wardenship, which I bestow on you in the name of the Turtle trust, will make perfectly clear to everybody both your value to the profession and your status in it.'

Clive raised his eyebrows. 'So the medical establishment embraces me fondly? Ah, well. I suppose if you can't fight 'em, join 'em.'

'The Warden's salary, though modest, will doubtless be a welcome supplement to your grant, and I expect you will pick up a lectureship before long. Luckily, I need have no misgivings about the future Mrs Moneypenny organizing the domestic side with skill and charm. Furthermore,' he added, tucking the handkerchief away. 'Anyone getting a bit uppish socially with you is going to have *me* to reckon with.'

'But I still don't grasp,' Clive continued, looking anxiously out of the window, 'why the high and mighty Wardenship should descend for my humble work on muscle metabolism?'

115

'Because of the nerve gas, you fool,' snapped Sir Lancelot.

'Nerve gas? What nerve gas?'

'Ye gods!' Sir Lancelot took out his handkerchief again. 'You mean you yourself didn't know the implications? I suppose you've heard of Colonel Lexington?'

'Lexington?' Clive frowned.

'You remember, darling,' Pat interrupted. 'He asked you to that reception and wanted reprints of all your papers.'

'Thank heavens we kept quiet about your despicable conduct today,' Sir Lancelot muttered, replacing the handkerchief. 'You will allow me to be utterly frank in the circumstances?'

Clive sighed. 'I can take my medicine.'

'You will understand I have grave personal reservations about your worthiness as Warden? To have even contemplated the act you did this very day renders you totally unfit for any post whatsoever in the country.'

Clive gave another frown. 'That's a bit hard, isn't it?'

'On the contrary, you should think yourself lucky you are not facing a judge and jury.'

'But there's no law against it,' Clive complained. 'And as long as Pat forgives me, that's all right.'

'Pat forgives you, by God! What about all your fellow countrymen and women?'

'Well, I'm not going to marry all of them,' Clive objected. 'And after all, you can hardly blame me. When Pat went and jilted me without even the four-minute warning I felt pretty bitter. Besides, it's terrible to be alone in London at Christmas. So I rebounded to Dublin to see this girl. She's called Fenella, and now she works at the Shelbourne. Nothing like a little Irish coffee to keep you warm on a December night,' he added.

'Good grief.' Sir Lancelot produced the handkerchief again. 'There's my speeding fines, for a start.'

Pat and Clive joined the party in Hall for Christmas Dinner. It was a great success, and the Chateau Lynch Bages was delightful. Afterwards, as everybody expected, Mr George Nightrider made a speech.

'In proposing this toast to the Warden of the Medical College,' he ended, after about twenty minutes, 'in this hospital so worthy of our National Health Service – which, as everybody knows, is the envy of all civilized communities – I would like to pay tribute to the gentleman among us tonight who made such a generous gift for the poor sufferers opposite in the wards.'

Cheers.

'I refer, of course,' added Mr Nightrider, in case anyone hadn't got the point, 'to Mr Shufflewell, and to his household. Believe me, I shall remember more than once his self-sacrifice, his thought of others, his charity and his compassion, once I find myself in the Min – minarets of Constantinople,' he finished obscurely.

'Ladies and gentlemen – ' Pop Shufflewell rose. 'I should like to propose a toast to Absent Friends.'

'Absent Friends!' roared everyone.

'There are many who are near and dear to us, Pop continued, 'but who, through force of circumstances, cannot be with us today.'

'Shame!'

'Our hearts go out to them in their separation from their families, and the good things of life we have enjoyed.'

'Hear, hear!'

'We can only look forward to that happy morn when we shall all be reunited together.'

'Most touching,' nodded Mr Nightrider.

'Excuse me, sir,' said a man in a mackintosh, appearing at his elbow, 'but we are police officers.'

'Why, there's Mr Anderson!' exclaimed Ma.

'Yeah, and Mr Jennings,' nodded Arnold.

' 'Ullo, Mr Anderson. Happy Christmas.'

'Happy Christmas, Mrs Shufflewell. Hullo, Milly. Had that long-expected baby yet?'

'And now,' announced Pop, finishing his glass, 'I shall have to be leaving you.'

'Oh, horror!' cried Mr Nightrider.

'Which one did you abscond from?' asked Sir Lancelot mildly.

'Hitchen Open. It's a piece of cake.'

'Oh, perfidy!' exclaimed Mr Nightrider.

'Ta-ta, all!' called Pop.

'Ta-ta, Pop! Take care of yourself.'

'See you in three years.'

'Oh, odium!'

'This looks like the stuff in the lorry he pinched,' added Mr Anderson, picking up a bottle of the claret. 'Do you mind if my sergeant here checks up on it, sir?'

'That photograph!' Mr Nightrider shot up. 'The papers!' He wiped his brow with his table napkin. 'What on earth will everyone think? Stolen property! And me about to be landed in the Min – minestrone,' he ended unhappily.

14

Clive Moneypenny and Pat were to be married in the local Registry Office on New Year's Day. Sir Lancelot, who never believed in doing things by halves, insisted on giving away the bride. He'd wanted to sport full morning rig and gardenia, but Clive insisted the ceremony was simple. He said he felt keenly sensitive to the resentment of the less well-to-do, now he'd become a Conservative.

'My dear, that looks quite delightful,' Sir Lancelot acknowledged, coming down that morning to find Lady Spratt alone in the Hall arranging a buffet for the reception. 'It quite makes me want to get married myself.' He slipped an arm round her waist. 'How would you like, my dear, to be going for a honeymoon with me all over again?'

'Not to Frinton,' she objected. 'It rained all the time.'

'Maud, I have a great surprise for you.'

She raised her eyebrows and shifted a plate of bridge rolls.

'I think, my dear, after thirty years of married life with me you deserve a change of scene. I have therefore decided, as I have no longer the Wardenship to detain me and I suppose Simon can handle my private practice, that we should go on a world cruise.'

'But Lancelot!' She smiled at him. 'What a simply splendid idea.'

'You deserve it, my love. And I fancy I might find those far-away places quite interesting, as long as one can get a decent steak in the evenings. So I should like you to go ahead and get the tickets,' he directed.

'Oh, I got them before Christmas.' She moved the crab sandwiches. 'We're leaving on the *Duchess of Gloucester* next Thursday week for six months. Stateroom Al, on the starboard side, handy for the swimming pool. Now I must go and pack that highly disorganized bridegroom's things for him. I really feel Pat has an uphill task ahead. You won't mind if he borrows a suitcase? Those airline people seem so hopeless, I doubt if Clive really remembered to put it on the plane at all. By the way, there's a visitor to see you.'

Sir Lancelot marched into his study, not at all pleased with the one-woman travel agency.

'What the devil are you doing there?' he barked, finding Arnold Shufflewell asleep in the big armchair.

'Oh, sorry, Guv'nor.' He got up. 'It's the weather. Fair wears you out. Very sensitive, I am, to the barometer, and that. I think I've got a very delicate skull,' he suggested, tapping it gingerly.

'Get out.'

'Got a letter for you, Guv'nor. From Pop. Smuggled out this morning. They got 'im in Wandsworth now.'

Sir Lancelot took the envelope.

'And Pop asked to tell you special, Guv'nor, how he enjoyed his Christmas. He says he hopes that letter will sort of repay you for the trouble. By the way, Guv'nor,' Arnold added, as Sir Lancelot tore it open, 'you wouldn't like to make a donation to the Prisoners' Aid Society?'

'Get out.'

'Right you are, Guv'nor. I'm only trying.' Arnold grinned. 'Funny ain't it, Pop ran the donations to charity game for years, except he always made it for 'ospitals.'

'Ye gods,' muttered Sir Lancelot staring at the letter. He rushed from the study. He ran across the hall. He threw open the front door as Randolph Nightrider was helping Susan Grantchester into his MG.

'Here, you drive this letter round to Simon Sparrow at my old Harley Street house immediately.'

Randolph stood on one leg.

'Won't you give a bloke a chance?' he managed to object. 'I've only just got the car fixed again, and I was taking Susan for a little run.'

'Don't keep answering me back,' snapped Sir Lancelot. 'And furthermore, you're not to go cutting fast and loose with that young woman. Kindly remember her mother is a lifelong friend of mine, and I shall be honoured with a degree from her hands this very afternooon.'

'Not cutting fast and loose,' mumbled Randolph Nightrider. 'Getting married.'

'Good grief! When?'

'As soon as he qualifies, Sir Lancelot,' smiled Susan.

'And no fast and loose till then,' added Randolph defensively.

'In that case I will congratulate you in advance on achieving possibly a lifetime's chastity. Now take that letter round and don't argue. Then collect my robes and things from the Staff Common Room,' he remembered. 'After the reception I shall be pressed for time.'

Randolph delivered Pop Shufflewell's note as Simon descended the steps of the Harley Street house. In his pocket was a cheque for five thousand pounds made out to Dr Defoe.

'Well!' Simon exclaimed, reading it. 'Perhaps this interview is going to be rather more pleasant than I expected.'

The vibration specialist was sitting behind a stylish desk in his dove-grey consulting room.

'I am glad you have such a sense of promptness, Mr Sparrow.' Dr Defoe gave a thin smile and shot his gold-laden cuffs. 'I will assist you in getting this faintly unpleasant meeting concluded as shortly as possible. I have a document from my solicitor acknowledging settlement of my claim. I assure you I will sign it as soon as you hand me the cheque, with my receptionist as witness.'

'Here's the cheque.' Simon produced it. 'It's made out to Dr Defoe. Is that right?'

'Perfectly.'

'You're sure you wouldn't prefer it made to Harry Driver?' enquired Simon. 'Or Terance Dupont? Or James O'Farrell? Or even Professor Wellbeloved?' he threw in generously,

The thin smile expired from inanition.

'What have you been up to?' he demanded shortly.

'I may not have friends in high places,' explained Simon, 'but I have them in useful ones. I appear to be indebted to a man called Shufflewell.'

'That old fool,' muttered Dr Defoe.

'You pulled a fast one on him in the past,' suggested Simon affably. 'Still, that's your affair. You can take me to court for slander as soon as you wish,' he conceded, 'and you'll probably win your case. But when I trot out from the witness-box those spells you did in clink for false pretences, it's not likely to help your practice. I think I should tread a little more warily in future, Defoe. If any other rich old ladies making wills start remembering you, so might the police. You'll probably get quite a good figure for the balance of your lease of these consulting rooms. Good morning.'

Simon tore up the cheque and scattered the pieces on Dr Defoe's desk. Then he decided to pick them up again and pocket them. In future, he felt warmly, he was going to be a pretty damn sight more careful.

'What's Sir Lancelot in such a tearing hurry for?' Professor Hindehead asked Paul Ivors-Smith in the main gate later that afternoon, as the retiring Warden came hurrying down the steps of the College. 'The wedding's all over isn't it?'

'He's off to the Senate House for his honorary degree,' Paul explained, while Sir Lancelot buzzed away in his bubble car.

'Oh yes, I remember. An odd business about the Wardenship,' he went on, as they turned to stroll across the courtyard towards the surgical block. 'Pity you didn't get it, Paul, though I suppose it will be a greater help to young Moneypenny. I had the Ministry of Defence on the phone again this morning. He seems to have struck on something rather fundamental.'

'As a matter of fact, sir,' Paul confessed, 'I could never have taken up the job anyway. You see, sir – I'm afraid I must ask you to release me by the end of the month. Dr Burton was on transatlantic phone last night with a simply splendid job in his clinic at Philadelphia.'

'Paul! You're not going just like that?'

'Afraid I am, sir. Apart from anything else, I want to get Deirdre away from London. Too many ghosts stalking round her, ever since we got married. She'll be much happier starting afresh in a new community in the States.'

'But this is terribly awkward,' complained the Professor, 'with me just starting my sabbatical year.'

'I know, sir. I'm sorry. But I expect one of the others will fill my shoes just as well.'

'Oh, very well, very well,' agreed the Professor testily. 'You can look after the department until you go, of course?'

'Naturally, sir.'

'You know where to get hold of me?'

'I don't think I've got the exact addresses.'

'There's a detailed list in my office. Don't forget to put clearly on the envelopes, 'Professor and Mrs Richard Hindehead, Passengers, First Class, *SS Duchess of Gloucester.*'

'I'll remember, sir. I hope you'll have an enjoyable six months' cruise.'

'I think we shall,' agreed the Professor, brightening a little. 'We have an excellent cabin – A2, on the starboard side, handy for the swimming pool. It should all be very interesting indeed.'

'My dear Sir Lancelot,' Elaine Grantchester greeted him in her Vice-Chancellor's robes at the back of the Senate hall. 'We were beginning to despair of you.

'A thousand apologies,' puffed Sir Lancelot. 'I was attending a wedding and as usual the bride was about five hours late. Moreover, some idiot – I mean, your daughter's fiancé – spilt an entire bottle of champagne down my suit. Fortunately, I have my morning clothes with my robes in my bag. Where can I change without creating a public scandal?'

'In my room, Sir Lancelot, of course. If you'll just pop your suit through the door, I can have the porter take it down to the cleaners in Oxford Street to be sponged and pressed. Then it'll be ready for the cocktail party at six.'

'That is very good of you, Elaine, very good of you indeed. I am only sorry this incident should mar my otherwise proud and unforgettable day.'

He plonked down his case in the Vice-Chancellor's room. Locking the door, he stripped himself quickly of his champagne-soaked lounge suit.

'Here you are!' he shouted, handing it outside at arm's length. 'Now look lively, or I'll never get it back at all.'

'Got my motorbike waiting, sir,' the porter assured him, hurrying off.

Sir Lancelot grunted. He locked the door again. Standing in his socks and briefs he drew one or two deep breaths. Best to compose oneself before appearing in front of all those people, he decided sternly. He flexed his muscles. Better now, he told himself. Perfectly cool, calm, and collected, he acknowledged. He crossed over and opened his suitcase.

As Clive and Pat Moneypenny decided to spend the start of their honeymoon at the Marlborough Hotel, they were alone in their room half an hour after the reception.

'I think the porter looked suspiciously at our luggage,' Clive laughed. 'But starting married life with so few possessions, at least we're spared lugging about a lot of heavy suitcases. And the one we're sharing doesn't even belong to us.'

'I wonder if yours will ever turn up from Dublin, darling?' asked Pat, unsnapping the locks. 'Look at this – !' she cried.

She held up the contents.

'A morning suit and a Doctor of Science's robes,' exclaimed Clive. 'How odd.'

But we must not intrude further into someone's honeymoon.

RICHARD GORDON

DOCTOR IN THE HOUSE

Richard Gordon's acceptance into St Swithin's medical school came as no surprise to anyone, least of all him – after all, he had been to public school, played first XV rugby, and his father was, let's face it, 'a St Swithin's man'. Surely he was set for life. It was rather a shock then to discover that, once there, he would actually have to work, and quite hard. Fortunately for him, life proved not to be all dissection and textbooks after all... This hilarious hospital comedy is perfect reading for anyone who's ever wondered exactly what medical students get up to in their training. Just don't read it on your way to the doctor's!

'Uproarious, extremely iconoclastic' – *Evening News*
'A delightful book' – *Sunday Times*

DOCTOR AT SEA

Richard Gordon's life was moving rapidly towards middle-aged lethargy – or so he felt. Employed as an assistant in general practice – the medical equivalent of a poor curate – and having been 'persuaded' that marriage is as much an obligation for a young doctor as celibacy for a priest, he sees the rest of his life stretching before him. Losing his nerve, and desperately in need of an antidote, he instead signs on with the Fathom Steamboat Company. What follows is a hilarious tale of nautical diseases and assorted misadventures at sea. Yet he also becomes embroiled in a mystery – what is in the Captain's stomach-remedy? And, more to the point, what on earth happened to the previous doctor?

'Sheer unadulterated fun' – *Star*

RICHARD GORDON

DOCTOR AT LARGE

Dr Richard Gordon's first job after qualifying takes him to St Swithin's where he is enrolled as Junior Casualty House Surgeon. However, some rather unfortunate incidents with Mr Justice Hopwood, as well as one of his patients inexplicably coughing up nuts and bolts, mean that promotion passes him by – and goes instead to Bingham, his odious rival. After a series of disastrous interviews, Gordon cuts his losses and visits a medical employment agency. To his disappointment, all the best jobs have already been snapped up, but he could always turn to general practice…

DOCTOR GORDON'S CASEBOOK

'Well, I see no reason why anyone should expect a doctor to be on call seven days a week, twenty-four hours a day. Considering the sort of risky life your average GP leads, it's not only inhuman but simple-minded to think that a doctor could stay sober that long…'

As Dr Richard Gordon joins the ranks of such world-famous diarists as Samuel Pepys and Fanny Burney, his most intimate thoughts and confessions reveal the life of a GP to be not quite as we might expect… Hilarious, riotous and just a bit too truthful, this is Richard Gordon at his best.

RICHARD GORDON

GREAT MEDICAL DISASTERS

Man's activities have been tainted by disaster ever since the serpent first approached Eve in the garden. And the world of medicine is no exception. In this outrageous and strangely informative book, Richard Gordon explores some of history's more bizarre medical disasters. He creates a catalogue of mishaps including anthrax bombs on Gruinard Island, destroying mosquitoes in Panama, and Mary the cook who, in 1904, inadvertently spread Typhoid across New York State. As the Bible so rightly says, 'He that sinneth before his maker, let him fall into the hands of the physician.'

THE PRIVATE LIFE OF JACK THE RIPPER

In this remarkably shrewd and witty novel, Victorian London is brought to life with a compelling authority. Richard Gordon wonderfully conveys the boisterous, often lusty panorama of life for the very poor – hard, menial work; violence; prostitution; disease. *The Private Life of Jack The Ripper* is a masterly evocation of the practice of medicine in 1888 – the year of Jack the Ripper. It is also a dark and disturbing medical mystery. Why were his victims so silent? And why was there so little blood?

'…horribly entertaining…excitement and suspense buttressed with authentic period atmosphere' – *The Daily Telegraph*

Printed in Great Britain
by Amazon

81889274R00078